I Do, I Don't

What Reviewers Say About Joy Argento's Work

Exes and O's

"I really appreciated the new take on a burned lover in Ali. Instead of pushing love away forever, she decides to actively seek out what has gone wrong in order to do better in her future. I also enjoyed how the story focuses on what a healthy relationship should be and how to get to that. It was refreshing. ...If you're in the mood for a gentle second-chance romance that has just enough angst, great character development, and will have you dying for a donut, run for this book!"—*Lesbian Review*

Before Now

"*Before Now* by Joy Argento is a mixture of modern day romance and historical fiction. ...There was some welcome humour and a bit of angst. An interesting story well told."—*Kitty Kat's Book Review Blog*

Emily's Art and Soul

"...the leads are well rounded and credible. As a 'friends to lovers' romance the author skillfully transforms their budding friendship to an increasing intimacy. Mindy, Emily's Down syndrome sister, is a great secondary character, very realistic in her traits and interactions with other people. Her fresh outlook on life and her 'best friend' declarations help to keep the upbeat tone."—*LezReviewBooks*

"This was such a sweet book. Great story that would be perfect as a holiday read. The plot was fun and the pace really good. The protagonists were enjoyable and Emily's character was well fleshed out. …This is the first book I've read by Joy Argento and it won't be the last. I'm looking forward to what comes next."
—*Rainbow Literary Society*

Visit us at www.boldstrokesbooks.com

By the Author

I Do, I Don't

by
Joy Argento

2023

CREDITS
EDITOR: CINDY CRESAP
PRODUCTION DESIGN: SUSAN RAMUNDO
COVER DESIGN BY TAMMY SEIDICK AND JOY ARGENTO

Acknowledgments

I would like to thank the readers who have taken the time to read my books and leave reviews. Your support has kept my fingers moving across the keyboard spitting out stories that would have made my brain explode if they didn't come out. Thanks for keeping my head intact.

Thank you to my editor, Cindy Cresap. Your words of encouragement mean the world to me.

Special thanks to Olessia Butenko, Julie Spelman, and Tobie Hewitt for finding all the mistakes that I miss. I am so grateful for you.

Thank you to my support system. You keep me going.

Susan Carmen-Duffy

Karin Cole

Georgia Beers

Barbara DiFiore

And my kids, Jamie, Jess, and Tony

Dedication

For Jackson

CHAPTER ONE

"No. No. No." Annie Jackson burst into Nicole Hart's office. "This can't be happening." Her dark brown hair whipped around as she shook her head. "I can't believe this."

The office was small, but it was all that Annie's production company could afford. Three small offices, Annie got the only one with a window. The third office was occupied by Lace, her twenty-something, pink-haired, tattooed assistant. They had access to the large conference room down the hall, as long as they booked it at least two weeks in advance.

"What's going on?" Nicole asked. She'd only known Annie a few months when she'd hired her to develop the algorithm for her new reality show *I Do, I Don't*. Annie was not only the producer, but she was also the director and editor as well.

"Bride number two backed out." She pulled the chair in the corner up to the edge of Nicole's desk and plopped down.

"What do you mean she backed out? She can't do that. She signed a contract. All of the pre-wedding interviews have been taped."

"Apparently, she got back together with her ex and she is no longer willing to marry a stranger."

"Oh shit," Nicole said.

"Exactly. The wedding is in less than two weeks. We can't afford to hold up production. We need to find another bride right away."

"Can't you sue her for breach of contract?"

"I could, but that wouldn't solve the immediate problem, not to mention the cost of a lawyer." Annie ran a hand through her hair, a habit Nicole had come to recognize when Annie was stressed. And this was certainly a stress-invoking development. "I need you to figure out who would be the next best match for bride number one."

Nicole had developed the algorithm that matched strangers with their best romantic possibility based on a series of carefully considered criteria, for the first lesbian dating-type show. But there was no dating involved. The two women chosen would meet for the first time at the altar and get married. Legally.

Annie alone had picked bride number one. Nicole didn't have access to real names or photos. Annie thought it was best to let her concentrate on the applicants' personalities, wants, needs, and deal breakers, when she fed the necessary information into the computer. With the first bride chosen, it had been Nicole's job to find her the best match from the forty or so women who had applied for the show. Hundreds had shown up for the initial call, but most left when they found out it wasn't exactly a dating show. Apparently, there weren't that many women willing to marry someone they'd never met. Nicole couldn't blame them. It was a crazy idea.

Both Annie's and Nicole's professional reputations were on the line. If the show failed, the whole project would be scrapped, not to mention that Annie had much of her life savings tied up in it.

"I need a list of the top ten matches for bride one. Can you have that on my desk by noon?"

"I can. I'll just have to pull the files. Annie, we'll figure this out."

"I'll have Lace contact the camera people and have them on standby to film the new bride's interview, along with her family and friends," Annie said. "We need to be on top of this. It could be a disaster if we aren't."

"I'll get right on it, Annie. We got this."

Annie went to the door and turned back to Nicole. "This could spell the end of our show if we screw it up." With that, she left, closing the door behind her. Nicole could hear her calling down the hall for Lace.

Nicole pulled up the compatible matches for bride number one. She removed the woman who was originally the top match, ran a new list, and printed it. There were no names, only numbers corresponding to a list of women that only Annie had access to. The original match, contestant number twelve, was a ninety-five-point match. The next woman in line, contestant number three, was an eighty-nine-point match. The rest of the list looked less than promising. Whoever contestant number three was had better agree to get hitched sight unseen to a stranger or they were screwed. They didn't have time to put out another call for possible participants.

Nicole double-checked the list, slipped it into a manilla folder, and trotted down the hall to Annie's office. Annie was on the phone in a very animated conversation, and Nicole stood in the doorway taking her in. Her wavy hair, several inches above her shoulders, was in disarray, and Nicole could only imagine how many times she must have run her hand through it.

Nicole had found her to be intelligent, capable, and very cute, with her square jaw, full lips, and dark brown eyes, when they'd met at Nicole's job interview. The dark-rimmed glasses she sometimes wore pumped up her appeal even more.

Annie spotted Nicole and wiggled a hooked finger at her. She pointed at the chair across from her desk. Nicole sat and slid the manilla folder across to her. Annie nodded and held up one finger.

"That was my lawyer," Annie said after finishing the phone call. "I wanted to keep her updated on the current situation." She pulled the list of applicants from the folder. Nicole had marked the ten top candidates for bride number one and their compatible traits. She scrutinized it. "It looks like there is only one woman on this list who is even close to being acceptable. Number three."

"Yeah. I saw that. If she doesn't agree to this, is it possible to change out bride one? I mean I know we would be starting from scratch."

Annie shook her head. "No. It's bad enough we have got to scrap all the footage we have on bride two. We don't have time to do both. Not to mention the fact that I chose her because she is beautiful, has a great personality and tons of charisma. She is the perfect woman to kick off this series. And we have a contract. We could be looking at a lawsuit. We need to do whatever it takes to make sure this woman, number three, agrees to be on the show. We need to get her booked today."

"I hear you. Anything I can do to help?" Nicole knew that Annie would handle contacting the candidate herself. She wouldn't trust anyone else with such an important task. Not to mention the fact that only Annie and the two-person camera crew were the only ones who knew who the brides were.

"No. I've got this." She shook her head. "Thanks."

Hiring Nicole to develop the computer program that matched the candidates for the show was a stroke of luck. Annie had interviewed at least a dozen people, and while some of them might have worked out okay, Nicole was head and shoulders above the rest when it came to her knowledge of what Annie needed. Her laid-back personality made working with her easy. Pleasant. The fact that she was beautiful didn't hurt. But Annie had put that on a shelf in the back of her mind. Thinking such things about an employee was just plain wrong. She barely noticed the way her long, dark blond hair had a bit of curl to it, or how her deep green eyes lit up when she accomplished some difficult task on the computer. She was off limits.

She kept her eyes glued to the papers in her hand as Nicole quietly exited her office.

"Number three," she said out loud. "Let's see who you are." She silently hoped she was good-looking. Like it or not, beautiful people made for better ratings.

Several keystrokes later, she pulled up the list of names, with corresponding pictures. "What the hell?" She was good-looking all right. Number three was Nicole Hart. She shook her head. Why was Nicole even on the list? This didn't make sense.

She called Nicole on her phone. Their budget didn't allow for intercoms. "Yeah. Can you come back to my office?"

Seconds later, Nicole appeared. "What's up? Problem with three?"

"Sit down, please."

Nicole did as she was told. "What is it?"

Annie turned the laptop toward her. "Number three. How is this possible?"

"Oh. When I developed the program, I put myself in as a placeholder."

"Explain. Please. I don't understand."

"I put my info in and then a couple of fake profiles. One with characteristics of my ideal woman and one with characteristics of someone I would have no interest in. That way I could see if it matched me with the right one. It did. I took out the two fake profiles but must have forgotten to take out mine. No big deal. I can take it out now."

Annie shook her head. "Is the information you put in for yourself true?"

"Yeah. Why?"

The deep breath Annie took to calm her nerves didn't help. "You're the next match," she stated simply. "And of course, that won't work."

"We'll just use the next person in line."

Annie turned the computer back around and typed. "Jessica Tetley is next in line. She is only a thirty-two-point match. That's not good enough. We promised our first bride someone who matched what she was looking for. Jessica is not it. What are we going to do? I'm at a complete loss here."

Nicole stood. "We're going to have to put out another call for contestants."

"We don't have time to do that. We need to get the new footage, all the interviews, and the outdated printed matter in the can in the next couple of days. We would need a complete background check on anyone new. And there's no guarantee we could even find a good enough match. The wedding venue is booked. There is no way they would give us a refund at such a late date. Besides, the first episode has got to be in the network's hands no later than September first. This could spell disaster for the show." Her job, Nicole's job, and quite frankly, a whole lot of money was on the line. She couldn't afford to shelve this.

"Um. Hmm. No time for another casting call. Jessica isn't a good enough match. Let me go back to my office and run the program again. See if there are any other women who would fit the bill."

"Are you telling me this list"—Annie held up the papers—"isn't accurate?"

"No. It's accurate."

"Then what is running the program again going to do?" Was the room getting hot or was it just Annie? Was it a hot flash? If so, it would be her first and not a normal thing for her to have at the age of thirty-seven. It had to be a panic attack. The fact that she was having trouble catching her breath sealed the deal. It *was* a panic attack. Darkness seemed to be creeping in from both sides of her vision. She closed her eyes against it and prayed she didn't pass out. This being her first panic attack, she wasn't sure how it would go.

"Are you okay?" Nicole asked. Her voice sounded farther away than across the small room. "Annie?" Nicole was next to her in an instant.

Annie opened her eyes to a spinning room. "Give me a minute."

"What's going on? Should I call someone? Nine-one-one?" Fear was evident in her voice.

"No. Just give me a minute," she repeated. She was sure a panic attack couldn't kill you. Well, almost sure.

"Okay," Nicole said. "Okay. Okay."

"What?"

"Okay. I'll do it."

"Do what?"

"I'll be bride number two," Nicole said.

So many emotions ran through Annie at once. Relief. Guilt. Fear. The feeling like she was going to throw up. The garbage can was within reach if that last one came to pass. She looked up at Nicole. The room was still spinning, but it was slowing down. "You can't."

"Why?"

"Because I can't ask you to do that. It wouldn't be right. And you work for me. How would that look?"

"We don't tell anyone that part. I've never seen bride one's picture. Hell, I don't even know her name. And I've put so many women's profiles into the computer that they all blur together. I have no idea who she is."

It was such a simple solution, and so complicated at the same time. She didn't want Nicole to do it. Didn't want her marrying a stranger. She wasn't exactly sure why. But now was not the time to try to unpack that.

"What other choice do we have?" she asked. Watching Annie in such a state scared the hell out of Nicole. She would have said just about anything in that moment to get Annie to snap out of it. She didn't really want to marry a stranger of course. She didn't want to marry anyone. Relationships had never been her strong suit. Marriage had been out of the question. Up until two minutes ago. She didn't see another way out of this mess. Her career—her dream job—was on the line, not to mention Annie's career. And she would do just about anything for Annie.

"I'll think of something," Annie answered.

"Divorce," Nicole said.

"What?"

"I only need to stay married for four months. Right? That's the premise of the show. You marry a stranger. Stay together for four months and if it doesn't work out, you get divorced."

"Yes, but why would you get married if divorce is on your mind?"

"It's not. It's just an option."

"I don't want you going into this unless you are really willing to give it your all. It's not fair to anyone if you don't."

"So, you'll consider letting me do it?" *For you.*

"Nicole, this doesn't seem right. This isn't a game. Bride one is a real person looking for her soul mate. You need to really think about this," Annie said.

Could she go into this and really give it her all? She let the idea roll around in her mind for a few minutes. The applicants had all become numbers and data to her. But Annie was right. There would be a real live flesh and blood woman she would be marrying. Would it be fair to her if Nicole was her bride?

It would be fairer than matching her with Jessica Tutley who wasn't a match at all. Yes. She could do this. For the sake of the show, bride number one, and of course Annie. She could give it her all. She just had to convince Annie. "I can do this, Annie. Do my best. Really try."

Annie seemed to think about it. Just when Nicole was convinced that she was going to say no, she nodded her head. "Okay. I don't think we have a choice. I'm not certain how else to do this. I'm going to ask you one more time. You're sure you want to do this?"

Was she sure? No. Not really. But she was willing and wasn't that enough? "I can do this."

"Okay," Annie said. "I'll start making phone calls to get things going. And who knows, it may just work. You wrote the program to match compatibility and you're a genius. So, if your program says you're a match it must be true. I think you and Li—umm, I mean bride number one would get along great. Remember, I've met her and her family. They're great. I can almost guarantee you won't regret this."

"Almost?"

"Is true love ever a sure thing?" Annie asked.

"I've never found true love. I believe in numbers and computer programs."

"Exactly. A computer program—your computer program—set this up. It can't be wrong."

Maybe Annie was right. Who knew what could happen? She still didn't think true love was for her, but she could be wrong. She hoped she was. "June wedding, right? Who hasn't dreamed about that," Nicole said with a laugh.

"It's not so much the wedding I'm worried about. It's the marriage part."

"Do you think it would be bad for the show if it doesn't work out?" She hadn't thought about that. She believed in the algorithm she created. She was determined to prove it worked. She just never thought she would be the one actually demonstrating it.

"Not at all. Of course, a happy ending would be great. And that still might happen. Don't count that part out yet. But with reality TV you never know what's going to happen. That's what keeps the audience tuned in." Annie was on her feet in half a second. She wrapped her arms around Nicole. "Thank you."

It had been a long time since a female other than her mother or best friend had hugged her. Nicole forgot how nice it could feel. Maybe spending time with someone wouldn't be so bad after all. Pretending to be married for the cameras—okay *actually* being married—could be okay. She could think of it as spending time with a friend. Surely, she and this woman—bride number one—could be friends. Maybe more. She wasn't sure if she hoped for that or not.

Annie was back in her chair almost as quickly as she had jumped up. She was back in business mode. "You need to get fitted for the wedding dress, set up a time to tell your family and whoever your closest friends are. I'll have the camera crew ready to film it all."

"Wait." A dress. She hadn't worn a dress in years. She was pretty sure it was her fifth-grade graduation. That stupid little ceremony where you walk across the stage with your parents looking on, bidding farewell to elementary school before moving on to middle school. Or torture school as Nicole remembered it. "I don't want to wear a dress."

Annie pulled back and looked in Nicole's eyes. "You don't have to wear a dress. Sit. Let's work out the details."

Nicole sat.

"A tux?"

"What?" Nicole asked.

"Do you want to wear a tux instead of a dress? We can do that."

Nicole hadn't thought that far ahead. "No. Not a tux. That doesn't seem right either."

"Well, naked would bring better ratings, but I'm not sure it's really an option." Annie laughed. She had visibly relaxed. "What do you propose? Propose." She laughed again. "See what I did there? Propose. It's a wedding show. Get it?" She was acting downright giddy. Nicole had never seen this side of her before. She wasn't sure if she liked it or not.

"We already bought the dress for the bride who backed out." Annie looked Nicole up and down. "I think you're about the same size. Maybe you could reconsider the dress idea. But I won't push. What do you think?"

Nicole tried to come up with an answer to her question, but her mind was whirling. Only one thought came through clearly. What had she just offered to do?

CHAPTER TWO

Jean and Sandy arrived at Nicole's parents' house about two minutes after she did. She had only met them once in passing at the office. There had been no reason to interact with the camera crew before now. They all had strict instructions to stay in their cars until Annie arrived. They didn't have to wait long.

"Okay," Annie said once they were all assembled in the driveway. "Jean is going to go in and film your arrival from inside the house. I'll be in there with her to direct things. Sandy will film from out here and follow you in. Are you ready?"

Ready to tell her parents; her brother, Ted; and his wife, Marley, who also happened to be Nicole's best friend, that she was getting married in less than two weeks—to someone she had never met? How could anyone be ready for that?

"Nicole? Are you ready?" Annie repeated.

"I don't think I can do this." Telling Annie she would do this was one thing. Telling her parents and the world that she was marrying a stranger. That was a whole other thing.

"What? Yes. You can. You got this. I'm right here with you." She nodded. "Nicole?" Was that panic in her voice?

Nicole had informed her family that a film crew would be arriving to film a segment for a TV show she would be appearing on. She knew they were confused but reassured them that she would explain everything.

"Nicole?" Annie said again.

Nicole took a deep breath and swallowed hard. "Okay. Just a moment of..." What? Fear? Dread? Remorse? She looked into Annie's eyes. "Nothing. Let's go. I'm ready."

Annie rang the doorbell. Nicole's dad answered the door. His thinning gray hair was combed back, exposing an ever-expanding forehead. Nicole was grateful he'd never done that comb-over thing some balding men did. Who did they think they were fooling? He had accepted his receding hairline with grace.

Annie extended her hand. "Mr. Hart. What a pleasure to meet you. I'm Annie. I understand Nicole told you we would be coming."

He shook the hand that was offered. "Yes. She did. I'm not quite sure what we're expected to do."

"Of course. Nicole will explain everything in a few minutes. Do you mind if Jean and I come in first? I have some release forms for you and your family to sign giving us permission to air the footage."

Nicole read the question in her father's eyes when he turned his attention to her.

"It's fine, Dad. I've looked over the contract. It's all on the up and up."

"Sure," her dad said to Annie. "If Nicole says it's okay, well, then I guess it is. Her mother, my son, and his wife are in the kitchen. Come on in." He held the door open as they passed. "Aren't you coming too?" he asked Nicole.

"I'll be in in a few minutes. Annie will let me know when she's done with the paperwork. They want to film me ringing the bell and entering. All the rigamarole. It's how they do it."

Her dad shook his head. "Television folks. I'll never understand it."

"Thanks, Dad." She gently pulled the door closed.

It seemed to take forever for Annie to open the door again. "All set. Give it about sixty seconds and then ring the bell. Your parents will answer the door together. Try to act as natural as you can."

Natural? There was nothing natural about any of this. Annie had given her key points to hit in the conversation but had left just how to do it up to Nicole. She'd been up half the night, various scenarios going through her head. She still hadn't decided exactly what to say.

Sandy tapped her on the shoulder. "Time to do this," she said and took a couple of steps back as she held the camera up to start filming.

Nicole rubbed the back of her neck to try to relieve the tension and rang the doorbell. *Act natural. Act natural.*

Just as Annie said, both of her parents were standing there when the door opened. She could just barely see Jean with her camera filming everything from inside the house. "Hi, honey," her mother said rather stiffly. "Come in. Ted and Marley are in the kitchen." Her father gave her a hug as if he hadn't just seen her ten minutes earlier.

She followed them in, with Sandy in tow. Without missing a beat, Sandy closed the door behind them with her foot. Obviously, this wasn't her first rodeo.

"Hey, sis," Ted called out as she entered the kitchen. Marley just nodded. They were seated at the small kitchen table, the one her parents had had since she was a baby. An extra chair had been pulled in from the dining room set. Everyone was dressed much nicer than the casual clothes they normally wore for family gatherings, and Marley had an extra layer of makeup on.

"Hi, Ted. Marley." Nicole nodded back. "Thank you all for agreeing to meet me here today." She pulled out a chair and sat. She invited her parents to do the same. Sandy and Jean stayed far enough back that they were out of the way and could get individual shots as needed. Annie stood off to the side, well out of the way of the cameras.

"What did you want to talk to us about?" her mother asked.

Nicole cleared her throat but didn't say anything. Annie made a rolling motion with her hand indicating that Nicole should start talking. She cleared her throat again.

Everyone's eyes were on her and she was hyperaware of the cameras, one aimed at her and the other seemed to be taking in the whole group.

"I...umm...well, ya see..." She stopped. This was much more difficult than she thought it would be. "I'm getting married," she finally blurted out.

"Married?" her father asked. "To who? I didn't even know you were seeing anyone. You didn't get back together with Stacy, did you? She didn't treat you right, honey."

Nicole almost laughed out loud. She hadn't thought about Stacy in months. There was no way in hell she would be marrying that psycho. "No, Dad. It isn't Stacy. I don't know who it is." There. She said it. Out loud. It was as real as it was going to get.

"I don't understand," her mother said. She didn't have her glasses on, which didn't surprise Nicole. She often took them off for photos so taking them off for a camera crew made sense.

"It's for a new reality show. *I Do, I Don't.*"

"You don't what?" her mother asked.

I don't want to be doing this, Nicole thought. She wasn't sure she had thought this through. She also knew it was too late to back out. "That's the name of the show. I've been matched with someone that I'm going to marry." She didn't feel like she was doing a very good job explaining this. "It's a matchmaking show. I'll be meeting my bride at the altar."

"That's just crazy," Ted said.

She couldn't argue with that. Annie had given her the words to say if someone responded like this. She was sure everyone was thinking it. Ted was just the first one to voice it.

"I believe in the process. I think this could be the person I've been hoping for. Dating hasn't worked out for me." Stacy. Exhibit A. "I'm almost thirty-two and I would really like to settle down with someone. I've been assured that we are a really good match. So, I'm going to trust this." She hoped her words didn't sound too rehearsed. "I'm hoping I have all your support."

Marley spoke up. "Of course, we support you. Right?" She looked around at everyone's stunned faces.

"Sure we do," Ted said. Nicole suspected that Marley had kicked him under the table, judging from the way he jumped.

"Marley, I'm hoping you'll agree to be my maid of honor," Nicole said.

"Of course. I would be honored to be your maid of honor." She laughed. It sounded forced.

"Matron," her mother said.

"What?" Nicole asked.

"She would be your matron of honor, because she's married."

Nicole rolled her lips in. She was telling them she was marrying a stranger and her mother was concerned with the proper titles. None of this made sense. She could see Annie in her peripheral vision, using her fingers to bring the corners of her lips up. Nicole forced a smile. "Thank you, Mom."

"We just want you to be happy. But this makes me nervous," her mother added. "When is this wedding supposed to take place?"

"June twenty-first."

"That's less than two weeks away. Are you sure you've thought this through?" Her mother's eyebrows went up so high, so fast, that Nicole thought they might fly right off her face.

"I have, Mom. I'm very sure about this. Dad, you haven't said anything. I'm really hoping you can be okay with this."

He shook his head. "You're my baby. I support anything you want to do. But how do you know what this person is like? That she's not crazy and will treat you right?"

"I've been assured that she has been well vetted. Thorough background check. The show would never put me in a dangerous position." Nicole could see Annie nodding her approval from the corner she was tucked away in.

The questions continued and Nicole did her best to answer them without revealing how she found herself in this position to begin with. When it was all over Jean filmed everyone giving Nicole a good-bye hug, leaving, and walking to her car.

Annie followed her out and Nicole rolled down her window. "We need to go back to the office and get the invitation list ready. I let your parents know the time and location of the wedding. You're going to need to call anyone you want to invite, at least twenty-five other people. We need all the seats filled. I've got actors standing by to fill in if we need them, but I would really rather have your actual friends there."

Oh shit. She hadn't even considered she would need to invite everyone she knew. She really was doing this. "Yes, boss," she responded.

"Hey. Don't do that. No one can know you work for me," Annie said.

"Sorry. You're right. I'll meet you back at the office." She had to wait for Annie, who had parked behind her, to pull out. She was half tempted to go back into the house and confess the whole sordid story to her parents. She'd always considered herself an honest person. It felt like she was lying by all the parts she'd left out. She didn't go back in of course. It would mean an end to the show, and her and Annie's careers, and she didn't want that.

"You did great," Annie told her once they were back at the office. "Make your list and start your phone calls. Give them as little information as possible. Make sure they know it's formal and no one under thirteen years old. The last thing we need is to have kids running around wreaking havoc. I'm going to call Marley and set up a time for her dress fitting. We'll do yours right before hers. I'm glad you agreed to wear the dress we already bought. That saves us a lot of money."

Nicole hadn't really agreed. She'd felt more like she'd been pushed into it. But what was one more uncomfortable thing in a whole line of uncomfortable things she'd almost begged to do? It was much too late to start second-guessing herself.

Annie waited for Nicole to respond and then returned to her own office. She seemed to thrive under stress, and this tight schedule was certainly cause for a lot of it. She called Marley, the wedding venue, the bridal shop, and the print shop to make sure everything was set. This was going to be a long day. Very long.

She couldn't afford, both financially and emotionally, to have this project fail. She'd never be able to face her parents again if she did. *Stupid* was the word her mother had used when Annie told her she was leaving her job as a producer for *Good Day Central New York*, the top-rated local morning show, to start her own production company. Her father, a man of few words, said he agreed. It seemed that only Terry, her older sister, was on her side. She would forever be grateful to Nicole for doing this.

Close to two hours later, Nicole knocked on her door and came in without waiting for Annie to respond. "Got all the calls made. I have twenty-two confirmed. I don't know who else to call to get that up to twenty-five."

"No problem. I'll have a few extras standing by. We don't want any empty seats. It doesn't look good on camera." And that's what all of this was about—how good everything looked on camera. Two beautiful brides, an outdoor event decorated to the hilt, and elegantly dressed guests would make this a show worth watching. It was like getting people's attention with bright, shiny objects.

"What's next?" Nicole asked, taking Annie out of her thoughts.

"Dress fitting tomorrow at noon. Marley will meet us there. You get a say in what she wears. The final decision rests with me. We have got to make sure it will translate to TV well."

"Of course."

"Nicole, I know this wasn't part of the plan when I hired you, but I so appreciate you doing it. We wouldn't have a show without you." It was the truth. She would forever be indebted to her. And who knows, Nicole and her bride might actually hit it off and live happily ever after. Of course, Annie was hoping for some good drama along the way. A few monkey wrenches thrown into the mix would keep the viewers coming back. If the brides didn't have any drama on their own, Annie was prepared to *make* it happen. Afterall, what was reality television without a few tears?

CHAPTER THREE

It was a beautiful day for an outdoor wedding. Annie was so glad there was zero chance of rain, and it wasn't so hot that everyone would be sweating through their formal wear.

Nicole was so stunning in her white dress, trimmed with lace, diamond drop earrings and matching necklace that it took Annie's breath away. The jewelry was on loan from a local store with a promise of a mention in the credits. "You look beautiful," Annie said. "And you're going to wear a hole in that carpet the way you're pacing back and forth."

"I can't help it," Nicole said. "I'm so damn nervous."

Annie resisted the urge to wrap her arms around her. "Your friends and family are here. Marley will be done with her makeup in a few minutes, and she'll be here. Everything is a go."

As if on cue, the door opened and Marley entered, dressed in a floor length royal blue gown. Her makeup was impeccable. The makeup artist Annie had hired did a wonderful job. Besides the brides and wedding party, she also did the makeup for the mothers of both brides.

"Wow. You look gorgeous," Marley said to Nicole.

"Right back atcha."

"How are you doing?"

"I feel like I'm going to crawl out of my skin."

Marley gave her the hug Annie had thought to do. But didn't. "Hey. It's going to be okay. This is what you wanted. To wear a beautiful dress, get married, and live happily ever after."

Annie knew that wasn't exactly the case, but she and Nicole had no choice but to follow through with this. Sandy and Jean were out filming the wedding guests. As soon as they got enough footage Sandy would be filming Nicole, and Jean would be focusing her camera on the other bride.

Lace arrived with Nicole's bouquet—red roses mixed with various other red flowers—and the printed vows that they'd worked on together. Annie had checked them over and given her approval.

"Set the flowers on the table," Annie told Lace. "I want Sandy to film Marley giving them to Nicole."

Once Sandy arrived and filmed what Annie wanted, Annie made her way down the hall to the other bride. Jean was already in the room filming the maid of honor getting the bride, Lisa Morgan, ready. She was as striking as Nicole. Almost.

Annie nodded at Lisa but was careful to stay out of the way of the camera. She waited until Lisa's best friend, Erin, finished adjusting Lisa's veil and handed her the bouquet, then signaled for Jean to get a close-up, and asked Lisa how she was doing.

"I can't believe this is real," Lisa said. "I've dreamed about my wedding day and even though I never really had a face to go with the fantasy I never thought I wouldn't have a face for real." She giggled. Annie had spent enough time with her to know she did that when she was nervous.

"You're going to be very pleased with the face that goes along with the reality," Annie assured her. "She's just about ready. Are you?"

"Ready as I'll ever be." Lisa took a deep breath.

"Good. Everything is set." They'd held two separate rehearsals, one for each bride, the day before with Lace standing in as a bride. Annie glanced at her watch. "We have just a couple of minutes and then we'll get you in position."

Annie made a quick phone call to Lace. "Everything's a go on this end. I'll get bride one there. You set to get bride two where she needs to be?"

"Yes. We'll be there in a couple of minutes," Lace replied.

"Great. Just enough time for Jean and Sandy to get where they need to be."

The guests were seated outside with Lisa's friends and family on one side and Nicole's on the other. Two small tents were set up behind the guests that would keep the brides separated until the ceremony.

She hung up, shooed Jean out to get ready to film, and got Lisa and Erin into position. This was really happening. Her vision was actually taking place. This was going to be a great show, and the network was sure to renew it and order a second season. That was the plan anyway.

❖

How the hell did I get myself into this? Nicole sucked her cheeks in nervously as they exited the building and made their way outside. She pulled at the back of her dress. The dress she didn't really want to wear. Lace led them to a small tent set up behind the rows of chairs where the guests were seated. It was situated in such a way that they couldn't see anything that was going on outside. That way Nicole couldn't see her bride until she was walking down the aisle toward her. Her bride. It all seemed surreal.

There was a matching tent set up on the other side of the yard. She would soon be married to whomever was hiding in there.

"I'm going to go get your father," Lace told her. "You'll be walking down the aisle soon." Soon. Too soon. Was there still time to run? The fact that Marley was tightly gripping her arm would make that difficult.

Lace returned with Nicole's dad in tow, smartly dressed in a black tuxedo with a red rose pinned to his lapel, just as the music started. Nicole couldn't see anything, but she assumed the other bride's maid of honor was walking down the aisle. It wasn't long before the music switched to "Here Comes the Bride."

Nicole's stomach dropped. The woman she was about to marry was out there, only feet away from her. She could hear chairs scraping as the guests rose to their feet. Her mouth went dry.

"We're up next," her dad said. "Ready, honey?" He offered her the crook of his arm.

Why no. No, I'm not. She nodded and slipped her arm through his. They waited for a change in music and Lace signaled for Marley to slip through the tent flap and make her way up to the archway.

The world blurred as "Here Comes the Bride" played again and her dad took a step forward. Nicole realized her feet weren't moving and she looked down wondering what was wrong with them.

"Honey?" her father said.

"Yep." Somehow, they were moving forward. Lace held the tent flap open, and they stepped out. Nicole blinked several times against the bright sunshine. It took her eyes a few seconds to adjust. At the end of the aisle stood a beautiful woman, dressed in white, holding a large bouquet exactly like hers. Several strands of dark hair peeked out from the white veil she was wearing. The skin on her heart-shaped face was flawless. Creases formed in the corners of her bright blue eyes when she smiled.

Nicole found herself smiling in return. Wow! Maybe I *can* do this. She was so focused on the woman in front of her that she didn't realize that her father had stopped when they got to the first row of chairs. He kissed her on the cheek and held her hand as she went up the two steps to the platform the woman was standing on. She glanced back at him as he took a seat in the front row next to her mother. Her mother had tears in her eyes. Why would she be crying at a fake wedding? No, not a fake wedding. A real wedding. A real wedding where she was marrying a beautiful woman she knew nothing about. Not even her name.

"Hi," the woman said shyly. "I'm Lisa."

"I'm Nicole. Nice to meet you." Nicole meant it.

"Will you marry me?" Lisa asked and giggled.

"Well, seeing we're both wearing white and there appears to be a person here ready to officiate, we may as well." Nicole smiled. Was it possible to like someone that you didn't even know? Apparently, it was.

"Are you two ready?" Phyllis, the officiant, asked. Nicole had met her at rehearsal the day before.

"Yes," they both responded.

"Welcome, friends and family. We are gathered here on this beautiful day to join these two women…" Phyllis glanced down at the paper she was holding. "Lisa Morgan and Nicole Hart, in marriage."

Nicole barely heard the words until it was time for Lisa to say her vows. "Nicole. I've waited for this moment most of my life. Standing here with you I can say it was worth the wait. I vow to you to be the best partner I can be. To put *us* above *me*. To learn your heart and to always listen to it. To take you as my wife."

Nicole was truly touched by her words. She seemed to say them with so much sincerity. Nicole looked at the vows in her hand and folded the paper in half. She took Lisa's hands in hers and decided to speak from the heart. "Lisa. I truly never thought I would find myself in this position, but in this moment I'm so glad I am. I promise to give this marriage all I've got." She surprised herself with the words that were coming out of her mouth. She wasn't sure what had come over her. It might have boiled down to lust, but Nicole didn't think so. And so what if it did?

She finished her vows, hoping they didn't sound too cheesy, and before she knew it the ceremony was done.

"I now pronounce you married," Phyllis said. "You may now kiss."

Lisa leaned forward and whispered, "Is it all right to kiss you?"

Nicole nodded.

Lisa kissed her lightly on the lips. It had been so long since Nicole had felt soft lips on her own. It felt nice. Really nice.

The ceremony wrapped up and Nicole took Lisa's hand as they walked together back down the aisle to the sound of applause. Nicole assumed the guests had been coached ahead of time to do that. Annie knew what made good television.

Lace met them at the end of their short walk and led them back to the room Nicole had gotten ready in. Jean followed with her camera fixed on them. "Congratulations, you two," Lace said. "Annie is going to talk to the guests. She'll be in here shortly. Make yourselves comfortable. There's a little bubbly and glasses on the table. Take a little time to talk and get to know each other before the reception."

With that, she left, and Nicole was alone with her wife. Well, alone with Jean and her camera. Wife. The word still seemed surreal. And why wouldn't it? They'd only been married for four minutes. She'd done it. She married a stranger. And at this moment she didn't regret it. That surprised the hell out of her. She hoped Lisa didn't regret it either. Nicole poured them each a glass of champagne and they settled down together on the love seat that just happened to be in the room.

Nicole took a moment to take in the woman next to her. Flawless skin, blue eyes with flecks of gold, dark hair that hung down well past her shoulders, and a smile that could kill you if you looked at it too long.

"Soooo," Lisa said, letting the word linger. "Should we talk or make out?" She let a long beat go by before adding. "I'm kidding. We don't even know each other. Of course, we shouldn't talk. What would we even talk about?" Her smile lit up her face.

Nicole laughed. "You're very funny." She liked funny. "Why did you want to do this?"

"I'm the adventurous type. What greater adventure is there than to get married? And marrying someone that I don't know, well, that just kicks it up a notch."

"Like bungee jumping into a marriage?"

"Something like that."

Nicole felt heat rising in her body. She prayed Lisa wouldn't ask her the same question. She didn't want to lie to her, but she couldn't tell her the whole truth either. Best to deflect. "Were you nervous?"

Lisa giggled and sipped from her glass. "Still am. You?"

Now *that* question Nicole could answer. "Extremely. I wondered if I was crazy doing this."

"And now?"

"Now I'm thinking this might be okay. I'm willing to try if you are." Nicole sipped her champagne and watched Lisa over the rim of the flute.

"I wouldn't be here if I didn't want to give this my all." Lisa took Nicole's hand. "I'm serious. I trusted the process. Annie assured me she had a great match for me. Now it's time to trust you."

Nicole tried to swallow down the pang of guilt that rose in her throat. Was she lying right from the start if she didn't admit that the *great match* had bailed, and Nicole had volunteered because she was second choice? It could be the end of everything if she said it out loud. The show. Her job. All the money Annie had invested in this. She couldn't do that. Best not to confess anything. "Let's make a pact to turn that nervousness into excitement," Nicole said.

Lisa smiled. "I like that plan."

"Hello, ladies. How are we doing?" Nicole hadn't noticed that Annie had slipped into the room.

"Great," Lisa answered. "I think everything went well. What do you think?" she asked Nicole.

"Same. You did a great job putting this together," she said to Annie. She almost added *on such short notice* but didn't.

"Thanks. Having such awesome brides helped. Anyway, we are all set for the reception. Are you two ready?" She gave them a quick rundown of what to expect. They went back outside, stopping just short of where the guests were gathered. Tables had been set up where the chairs had been. The caterers were busy setting out trays of food on a long table at the edge of the lawn. A band set up off to the side boasted a singer, a guitar player, keyboards, and drums. Annie gave them a signal and the singer stepped up to the mic. He tapped on it twice. "Ladies and gentlemen, can I get your attention please?" He waited until virtually everyone had turned their attention toward him. "I'd like to present for the first time as a married couple, Lisa and Nicole." He waved his hand in their direction.

Nicole felt heat rise to her face. She was not one who liked attention. Lisa took her hand, lacing their fingers together. She didn't seem to mind everyone looking at them. Annie gave them a little push from behind. Nicole plastered a smile on her face and stepped forward with Lisa to a smattering of applause. Nicole searched the crowd for her people, spotting several smiling friends. Her gaze finally fell on her parents. Her dad had his arm around her mother's shoulder almost as if he was supporting her. Nicole hoped this whole ordeal hadn't been too hard on them. She knew they only wanted the best for her, and if she knew her mother at all—which she did—she would be worried about Nicole's heart, and probably her sanity. Nicole had questioned her own sanity repeatedly over the last week and a half. What kind of a person married someone before they even met them? Lisa did that willingly and she seemed pretty sane, at least in the thirty minutes Nicole had known her. She suppressed the laugh that bubbled up in her throat. She was married. Married. To someone she now knew for less than an hour. If that didn't fall under the category of insane, she didn't know what did. Almost as if on cue, Lisa squeezed her hand. The guests parted to let them pass.

The band was playing, and the guy at the mic was singing "Strangers in the Night." How appropriate and ironic. Lisa pulled Nicole into her arms, and before Nicole realized what was happening, they were dancing. It felt both comfortable and extremely strange. They danced with just enough distance between them that if this had been a high school dance—which Nicole had never attended—they would have been deemed acceptable.

"How ya doing?" Lisa whispered.

"Hanging in there. You?"

"You're a very good dancer."

"That's only because you're so good at leading."

Lisa giggled. "I didn't realize I was leading."

The song came to an end, and the guests that had circled around them clapped.

"If everyone would please take your seats, someone will be around to each table to let you know when it's time for your table to go up to the buffet."

The head table became visible as the guests shuffled to their assigned seats, marked with a place card. Lisa led them to their place. Marley and Lisa's maid of honor were already seated one on each side of where the brides' seats were.

Nicole pulled out the chair for Lisa. She was nothing if not chivalrous. She noticed Jean in front of them filming and Sandy off to the side getting them from a different angle. They had been doing a great job of staying out of the way.

"You doing okay?" Marley asked her once she was seated. Everyone seemed to be asking her that. Did she not seem okay?

"Fine." Nicole didn't really know what she was feeling. Or maybe she was feeling everything all at once. It was hard to decipher.

The rest of the day was pretty much a blur. Eating. Dancing. Guests tapping silverware on the side of their glasses to get the new couple to kiss. The first couple of times Nicole didn't mind it. By the third time it was annoying.

"Now that you've made your rounds thanking everyone for coming, the limo is all set to take you to the honeymoon suite at the Hotel Belvedere. Your overnight bags are already there. Jean is going to ride with you and film from within the limo. Lace is going to be driving Sandy and follow behind you to film the car ride. Once you get to the hotel, both Jean and Sandy will follow you in. They'll film from different angles but have orders to stay out of your way."

It was only the first day and Nicole was already tired of being followed and having her every move recorded. How in the hell did reality stars do this all the time?

"Once you retire for the night, Sandy will be in the bedroom with you." Annie made eye contact with Nicole and read the silent question that must have been on her face. "Yes. You are expected to sleep in the same bed. Sandy will stay for about ten minutes after you get into bed. Then it's lights out as far as the cameras are concerned, and what you do from there is up to you."

Small pecks on the lips with a stranger was one thing. Sleeping with—making love with a stranger—that was something Nicole had never done and wasn't keen on the idea now. She hoped Lisa wasn't expecting that either.

"The cameras will pick you up again about eight tomorrow morning. If you aren't up yet, Sandy will let herself into your suite and start filming the second you come out of the bedroom. It's up to you if you want to freshen up first or come out with no makeup and your hair in disarray."

Nicole hadn't realized the extent of the cameras intruding on her life. She wasn't sure she could deal with it.

"Feel free to order room service for breakfast. I'll be there around ten for an after-the-wedding night interview—with the cameras running, of course."

Nicole had never heard Annie talk so much before. She wished she would just stop now. It was all too much to take in.

"I expect honest answers to anything I ask, but it's up to you how personal you want to get. You don't need to reveal everything that transpired during the night." Nicole half expected her to wink at that. She didn't.

"We got it," Nicole said, trying to get her to shut up.

"Okay then." Annie gave each of them a hug. "Have a good night. And I'll see you tomorrow. You both did great today."

Nicole was surprised that Annie didn't pull her aside to give her further instructions. Relief washed over her when she didn't.

Lisa took her hand, and they made their way to the parking lot and the waiting limo, followed closely by Jean, Sandy, and Lace.

They were relatively quiet on the ride to the hotel. Nicole wondered if Lisa was as wired and tired as she was. The look on Jean's face told her she was disappointed there wasn't more going on to record.

The hotel suite was spacious, with a sitting area, small kitchenette, bedroom, and two bathrooms. Nicole and Lisa took turns in the bedroom to change out of their wedding attire. Nicole felt so much better in her jeans and T-shirt. She sucked in a breath when Lisa emerged wearing light blue jeans and a black tank top. As beautiful as she had looked in her wedding dress, Nicole thought she looked even better in her casual wear.

There was a bottle of champagne in a bucket of ice and a large bouquet of flowers next to it on the small table against the wall. "Would you like me to open that?" Nicole asked Lisa, pointing to the bottle.

"Not for me. You go ahead if you would like some."

Nicole wasn't a big drinker, and the three glasses she'd had at the reception were enough to hold her over for a while.

They settled down together on the couch, Nicole hyperaware that every word, facial movement, and action was being recorded.

"Tell me about yourself," Lisa said. "I thought your parents and brother were very nice. And your matron of honor, Marley, I'm assuming she's your brother's wife?"

"Yes. They met through me. She was a casual friend, but we got much closer after she joined the family."

"What do you do for a living?"

Nicole needed to tread carefully. *Be honest, but don't give away too much.* Of course, if this worked out, she would confess everything at the end of the four months, when the cameras stopped rolling. "I design computer programs for a small local company and occasionally freelance for larger ones." Although she hadn't freelanced since she started working for Annie. She found herself too busy and her salary was enough that she didn't need the extra money freelancing provided.

"That's cool. I'm a kindergarten teacher. I love kids. I'm hoping we can agree to have a big brood. Maybe six or seven."

Nicole swallowed. Hard.

Lisa let out a giggle that Nicole was already finding cute. "Relax. I'm just kidding. I'm not against having kids, but I'm in no rush. What are your thoughts?"

Nicole laughed. Relieved. She hadn't ever really thought about having kids. She'd had no intention of ever getting married so she figured kids wouldn't be in the picture either. She made a mental note to tweak the computer program to add more importance to the question of whether or not someone wanted kids. She was pretty sure she checked *Not Sure* when she filled out the form. She assumed Lisa had checked the box that said *Yes I Want Kids*. Future applicants would need to match on this point, or they shouldn't be paired up. It was a stupid mistake on her part. One she needed to correct. "I've always wanted nieces and nephews," she answered honestly. "I guess I would consider it."

Lisa shook her head. "I'm sorry. We've just barely met. I shouldn't have even asked you that."

"Why not? If we had been dating before jumping blindly into marriage, we would have discussed it. We are doing everything backward here, but no question should be off the table. It's the only way to get to know each other."

"Thank you for saying that. I don't want to overstep."

"The truth is I hadn't really thought about having kids. I know that's kind of strange. By the age of thirty-one—almost thirty-two—I guess most women would have decided if they wanted kids or not by now."

"When?"

"When what?"

"When will you be thirty-two? When's your birthday?" Lisa asked.

"Oh. August twenty-second."

"You're on the cusp."

"I beg your pardon?" Nicole raised her eyebrows.

"Your zodiac sign. You're a Leo, the lion and it's the last day for that. August twenty-third starts Virgo, the virgin. You don't know zodiac signs?"

"Not really, but I'm glad I'm a lion and not a virgin. Missed that one by a hair." Nicole held up her hand, her thumb and forefinger close together.

Lisa laughed. "You did. If you had been born a month earlier you would have been a Cancer, the crab."

"Again. Glad to be a lion, and not have cancer or crabs." Nicole smiled.

Lisa returned it. "You wouldn't have cancer or crabs. At least I hope you don't have crabs. I do believe Annie did a thorough background check, but I don't think it was that thorough."

"No. She did not check for that."

"You're a fire sign. Vivacious, a bit theatrical, and passionate. Some Leos like to bask in the spotlight. Any of that fit you?"

"Oh my God. No. I'll have to ask my mother if she lied about my birthday."

"Not passionate?" Lisa asked.

"I guess that part is right. But I hate the spotlight. And I don't bask."

"And yet you just got married on national TV. You are quite the contradiction, Nicole Hart."

Lisa shifted her weight on the couch and pulled her legs up under her.

Nicole appreciated how relaxed she seemed. She wished she could relax more, but her nerves were still somewhat on edge. "What's your sign?" Nicole asked.

"Pisces, the fish. Water sign. Intuitive. Imaginative. Creative. Compassionate and sensitive. I would say that pretty much fits me."

"Good to know," Nicole said. "You're water and I'm fire. Do those things mix?"

"Oh yes. Together they make steam." Lisa wiggled her eyebrows.

"Hmm. And your birthday is in…?"

"March fourteenth. And before you ask, I'm thirty-four."

"I wasn't going to ask," Nicole said. "Okay, I was. But I was trying to figure out the best way to do it."

They talked for the next few hours. Nicole learned about Lisa's family, her childhood, and her job. She shared much of the same with her. When the conversation started to wind down, Lisa suggested they turn in for the night. Lisa got ready in the bathroom and Nicole in the bedroom. She slipped under the covers as soon as she had her two-piece pajama set on. She bought it online, having no idea what would be appropriate. She slept in a long nightshirt sans underwear at home.

Lisa emerged from the bathroom wearing a frilly floral nightgown that stopped just above her knees. Nicole wondered if she had underwear on. Tonight wouldn't be the night to find out. She wanted to get to know Lisa before letting that happen. She wasn't sure how Lisa felt about that. It was one thing they hadn't discussed. There was no way Nicole was going to talk about intimacy with the cameras rolling.

Lisa had just slipped into bed when there was a knock on the bedroom door. "If we ignore that, do you think they'll go away?" Nicole asked.

"Probably not." Lisa turned toward the door. "Who is it?"

Nicole laughed.

"It's Sandy," Sandy said through the door. "Are you dressed? I have strict orders from Annie to film in the bedroom for a little while."

Nicole groaned. "Guess there is no getting around this," she said to Lisa. "The quicker we let her in the quicker she'll leave."

"Come in," Lisa called.

"Sorry," Sandy said. "I know this is a delicate time. But boss's orders."

"I get it," Nicole said. And she did.

"Do whatever you were going to do." A blush creeped up Sandy's pale neck to her freckled face. It was a shade or two lighter than her red cropped hair. "But don't take it too far while I'm here."

Lisa rolled over and faced Nicole. "You were going to tell me the story about having six toes on one foot and no toes on the other."

Nicole burst out laughing.

"Come on. Annie is going to kill me if I don't get any good footage," Sandy complained. "Can you kiss or something? I'm sure Nicole's toes are just fine and normal. I saw her feet when she took off her shoes at the reception."

"Did you get good footage of my feet?" Nicole asked her. "That way we can attract a fetish following as well."

Sandy shook her head and Nicole could tell by the look on her face she was frustrated.

"Okay. Okay." Nicole put her hand on Lisa's bare arm and ran it up and down her silky skin. She waited for the tingle that she expected to invade her center, but it didn't come. She probably needed more time to get to know her. "I can't believe we're married," she said. Nicole knew what kind of footage Annie was looking for. "You're so beautiful." She could give Annie what she wanted and still be honest. Lisa was beautiful.

"You are too," Lisa responded. "I wasn't sure what to expect, but I can say I was very pleased when I saw you walking down the aisle toward me."

"Me too." They made small talk until Nicole yawned. "I'm ready to turn off the lights. How about you?"

Lisa nodded. Nicole kissed her lightly on the lips, reached over to the nightstand and turned out the lights. She waited a minute and turned it back on. "Got enough?" she asked Sandy.

"Yes. Thank you. I'll be on my way. I'll be back at eight tomorrow morning. If you aren't up yet, I'll just wait in the sitting area." She closed the bedroom door on the way out.

It was the first time Nicole was truly alone with Lisa. She wasn't sure what Lisa was expecting of her, and she wasn't sure how to open the conversation.

"Umm, I know it's our choice what happens tonight," Lisa said before Nicole had a chance to say anything. "How would you feel if we wait to be intimate? For me personally it means so much more when I have feelings for someone. Not that I don't like you," she added quickly. "I mean, I like you, but what I mean is…" She seemed to be stumbling over her words.

"I feel the same," Nicole said. "I would rather wait, too."

"Oh good," Lisa said. "I was so afraid I was going to offend you."

"I was worried about the same thing. After all, Pisces are the sensitive ones."

Lisa smiled. "True."

Nicole breathed a sigh of relief. She turned out the light. "Good night, Lisa."

"Good night, Nicole."

No lovemaking that night. But tomorrow was another day.

Chapter Four

Annie pulled the covers back on her queen-size bed and climbed in. Alone. She would have gotten a dog or cat long ago, but her excessive work hours would be so unfair to a pet. She thought back to the events of the day. Everything had gone off without a hitch. The wedding was beautiful, as were both brides.

Nicole looked especially gorgeous in her white dress and her hair hanging down in soft curls framing her face. If she was being honest with herself—and she always tried to be—she was jealous of the adventure that awaited them.

She would have loved to be curled up in bed with someone she adored. Her love life had taken a back seat to her career. Not that she regretted it. Mostly. It had been a long time since she'd enjoyed the company of a woman.

Nicole and Lisa were free to do whatever they were moved to do tonight. Annie knew what she would be doing if it was her there instead of Lisa. She didn't know if they would share any intimate details in the morning. She wasn't sure she wanted to hear them if they had made love. It would be great for ratings. And that's what her life seemed to revolve around these days. Chasing ratings.

She was *usually* happy with the life she'd carved out for herself. She wondered why she was feeling so lonely now. Maybe it had to do with the wedding and watching two people become a couple. Maybe it was… She didn't know.

She grabbed her iPad from the nightstand and went through the list of questions she would be asking Lisa and Nicole in the morning.

Nicole valued honesty, and Annie knew that keeping the fact that she worked for the show from Lisa wouldn't be easy for her. But telling Lisa would destroy everything. There was way too much on the line. She also knew that the closer they got, the harder it was going to be for Nicole. She could only hope Nicole would be able to keep that information under wraps.

She changed the wording on a couple of the questions and threw her iPad on the other side of the bed. The side that no one was sleeping on. Another reminder that she was alone.

"Alexa," she said to the unit on the nightstand. "Set an alarm for seven a.m."

"Alarm set for seven a.m.," Alexa told her.

"Alexa," she repeated. "Do you love me?"

"I don't have human love figured out quite yet," Alexa responded.

"Me either." Maybe that was why she wanted to make this show. Love. Wasn't that the end-all and be-all for some people? She didn't know what that was all about. Deep down she hoped this show, *I Do, I Don't*, would help her figure it out. And maybe somewhere along the line she could find some love of her own. But she doubted it.

❖

Seven o'clock in the morning came way too quickly when you tossed and turned most of the night. "Alexa, stop." The alarm ceased. "I thought you were my friend."

"Playing 'Thought You Were My Friend' by Magic Dagger," Alexa responded and some song that Annie didn't know started to play.

"Alexa, stop," Annie said much louder than necessary. She crawled out of bed and downed a strong cup of coffee before her shower.

Nicole and Lisa had just finished breakfast when Annie arrived. Sandy was there recording everything. Annie was pretty sure she would be editing most of it out, unless there had been some very interesting conversation going on.

"Good morning, ladies. I trust you had a restful night."

"Restful. Yes," Nicole said with a smile.

Annie wasn't sure if she was toying with her or being truthful. There was that pang of jealousy again. What the hell? "Jean should be here any minute and we can get started. I'll have you both stay to answer the first round of questions. Then we'll do one at a time."

A minute later, there was a knock on the door and Jean came in, using the key card Annie had made sure that both camera women had. Annie positioned everyone and they got started. She lobbed them some softball questions to start. *How are you feeling? How do you think yesterday went? Were you happy with the turnout?*

She asked Nicole to take a walk for about thirty minutes and directed her next set of questions to Lisa. "What was your first impression of Nicole when you saw her?"

"Oh my God, she is beautiful. I was very happy. I just hoped that her heart was as beautiful as the rest of her."

Annie couldn't help but smile. The short time she'd known Nicole she knew how kind and thoughtful she could be. She often went above and beyond at work. Case in point—stepping up to replace their absent bride. "I know it's only been a day, but what do you think of her heart so far?"

"So far, so good. We've had some nice chats and she really seems like she's very understanding and caring."

"You think it's a good match?"

"Yes. I'm very pleased. Only time will tell if it's a match made in heaven or if it's not meant to be."

Annie wasn't sure which she wished for. Conflict and strife would be just as good for ratings as a happy ending. Although she couldn't imagine Nicole causing discord. "What are you hoping happens going forward?"

"Love, of course, would be the ultimate goal." She laughed. "We already have the marriage. I look forward to getting to know Nicole better. Much better."

She asked a few more questions hinting—but not outright asking—if they'd had sex. Lisa was very good at answering the questions without answering *the* question. That was okay. It would keep the viewers guessing. Annie was guessing no. Nicole didn't seem like the kind that would jump into bed with someone without some sort of feelings attached. She'd interviewed Lisa several times before choosing her for the show. She got the impression that she had no trouble with intimacy, but having sex with someone she'd just met, even if she liked her, might not be something she was into either.

Nicole returned and it was Lisa's turn to disappear for half an hour. Annie asked her the same questions and she got similar answers except for one. "What are you hoping happens going forward?"

"I'm hoping we both end up happy, no matter how this plays out."

Annie wasn't surprised. As far as she knew Nicole hadn't been looking for a lifetime partner before this.

They finished with about ten minutes to spare. Annie addressed Sandy and Jean. "Cut the cameras and take a twenty-minute break. There's a café on the ground floor. Go grab a cup of coffee or a snack or something."

"How are you really doing with all this?" Annie asked Nicole once they were alone.

"I'm doing okay. It's not bad. Lisa is great so far. I don't know how I'll feel when it's time for real intimacy. I mean I'm not a prude, but it changes things. You know? I wouldn't want to hurt Lisa if she gets attached and I'm just not feeling it. I'm not sure I'm explaining this very well."

"No. You are. I get it. Sex makes you feel closer. There can be certain expectations after that happens."

So that answered that question. They didn't have sex and it seemed like Nicole wasn't in any kind of hurry to get there. Why was Annie happy with this revelation? It didn't make much sense.

Nicole wasn't against having sex with Lisa. She'd had one-night stands with women she barely knew. But that was in the past and there had been no expectations from either side. This was a whole different story. She hadn't expected to sign up for this, but Lisa did. The last thing she wanted was to hurt her. This whole thing didn't seem fair to either of them. Was it possible that they would fall in love and get the happily ever after that Lisa hoped for and Nicole never thought possible? She liked Lisa. She was easy to talk to and they seemed to have some things in common, but Nicole knew from past relationships that you really couldn't tell after such a short time. A few of her relationships had started out so promising only to crash and burn and leave Nicole to pick up the shattered pieces. That was why she didn't really believe in love. She hoped she was wrong.

"You seem hesitant," Annie said as if reading her mind.

"Love has always eluded me. I find it hard to believe that being thrown into this situation would end with it."

"I've met your parents. They seem like they really love each other. Am I right?"

"Yes." Nicole wasn't sure what Annie was getting at.

"That doesn't prove that love is real and attainable?"

Nicole laughed and shook her head. "My brother found it too. He and Marley were made for each other. But that doesn't mean there is a soul mate for me. My history isn't pretty."

"Maybe you've just put your faith in the wrong people. This time you're putting your faith in me—and the computer program *you* designed. I think the odds are in your favor." Somehow the words didn't match the look on Annie's face. Nicole couldn't quite read it.

"I'm here. I'm married. I'm willing to see where this goes." Nicole grinned. "I did design a hell of a good program. Algorithms are my jam."

"You did." Annie returned the smile.

Nicole turned when the door opened. Lisa stuck her head in and whispered, "Okay to come back?"

"Yep," Annie answered.

"Where are the cameras? I almost feel weird without them."

"On a break," Annie answered her. "Come on in and have a seat. I want to fill you in on your honeymoon, and we need to make some decisions."

"Ooh. A honeymoon," Lisa exclaimed and rubbed her hands together.

"What kind of decisions?" Nicole asked.

"Where you're going to live. When you are both expected to go back to work. If cameras are allowed where you work. Things like that."

Nicole was pretty sure cameras would not be allowed to film her where she worked. That would blow this whole thing out of the water. Just the thought of that made her breakfast threaten to come up.

"Where are we going on our honeymoon?" Lisa asked. "Hawaii? Paris? Ooh, Italy? I've always wanted to go to Italy."

Annie laughed. "Me too. Not this time. Sorry. Niagara Falls. Being a brand-new show the budget isn't as high as we would like. I did however get you a driver, so you don't have to worry about getting there. Have either of you ever been there?"

"My parents took me when I was a kid," Nicole said. "But I don't remember much."

"I haven't," Lisa said. "Isn't that usually the way? People come from all over the world to see it and we live in the same state and never get there."

"Well, you're going now." Annie pulled a folder out of her briefcase and handed it to Lisa. Here is your itinerary, dinner passes, spending money, and such. I expect a decent souvenir."

Nicole laughed. "For sure."

"Have you two discussed where you're going to live?" Annie pulled a yellow legal pad and pen from the briefcase.

Nicole hadn't even considered that. She hadn't let her brain get much past the thought of getting married. It would only make sense that they live together. She felt stupid for not realizing it.

"We haven't," Lisa volunteered. "I was kind of hoping we could live at my place. I have a dog." She turned to Nicole. "I hope you like dogs. I had that as one of my needs on the form I filled out."

"I do." It was those two words that got her into this to begin with. Now she was looking at the possibility of not living in her own apartment for at least four months. Should she suggest they live in hers? No, that wouldn't work. Dogs weren't allowed. This stuff should have been worked out up front. Going forward, she would have to make sure there were questions addressing this on the forms the applicants filled out. She and Annie had dropped the ball on this one.

"Where do you live?" Nicole asked.

"I don't usually give out my address on the first date, but considering we're married, I guess I can tell you." Lisa giggled. "I own a house in North Syracuse. Elmwood Ave. Does that work for you?" She smiled. Perfect teeth surrounded by perfect lips.

How could Nicole say no to that face? "Sure. I can do that."

"Not too far from work?" Lisa asked.

Annie scribbled some notes on the legal pad.

Nicole avoided looking at Annie. "No. It should be an easy drive." As far as Nicole knew, Lisa had never been to the office. Not that she would be going now. Annie had rented a conference room at a local hotel for the initial interviews with the promising applicants and the follow-up ones in their homes.

"Great. That's settled. Jobs. Lisa, I assume you told your employer you were getting married. When are you expected back?"

"Not till September."

Annie ran her hand through her hair. "That's right. You're a teacher. I can't believe I forgot that."

Nicole couldn't believe it either. Annie always seemed to have her act together. "I have a week and a half off," Nicole said before Annie asked her. Not that Annie didn't already know that. Even that was stretching it. She had so much work to do to narrow down the women for the second season. The plan was to start filming the new couple a month after Nicole and Lisa's four months were up.

"Lisa, have you spoken to your boss about the possibility of having the cameras follow you at work?"

"I have. They can be in the teachers' room but not in the classroom."

"Totally understandable." Annie said, writing on the pad. "And Nicole?"

"My boss is a real..." She let the words drift off.

Annie stopped writing and looked up. "A real what?"

Nicole smiled. "A real great person. I like her a lot, but she feels it would compromise the projects we're working on."

"Okay then. No cameras. We can deal with that. Is it all right if I grab a bottle of water?"

"Of course. Make yourself at home. Our hotel room is your hotel room. Literally," Nicole answered.

Annie went to the small fridge in the kitchenette and grabbed a bottle of water. "Would anyone else like something to drink? Water? Soda? I see you didn't open the bottle of champagne. Shame to let it go to waste. Shall we open it and add some orange juice? We can toast to the new couple with mimosas."

Nicole shrugged. "Sure. Why not."

Annie found orange juice in the small refrigerator and made the drinks. She held up her glass. "To many years of happiness."

Years? Nicole had made it through one day. Four months seemed like a very long time. Years seemed like forever. But forever with Lisa might not be so bad. She smiled to herself.

The drive to Niagara Falls was uneventful. Sandy sat in the front seat with the camera trained on Lisa and Nicole in the back for the whole two-and-a-half-hour drive. Nicole wondered how she could hold the camera up that long. She felt the urge to feel her arm muscles. They must be amazing.

Their hotel room was just that. A room. With a bathroom. It was an older hotel, with several coats of paint on the trim and baseboards, but at least it was clean. Sandy had a room next door. God forbid she not be available to record every waking moment.

Nicole wouldn't be surprised if she snuck in and filmed them while they were sleeping as well.

They had barely settled in when there was a knock on the door. "Sandy," Nicole said to Lisa. "Should we pretend we aren't here?"

"Do you think that would work?"

There was another knock. Louder this time.

"Nope."

Lisa went to the door and opened it. "I just need to set this up," Sandy said, holding up a tripod with a camera on it. She made her way into the room and set about putting it in place.

"Does this mean you're not going to be hanging with us?" Nicole asked, hoping the answer was yes.

"Nope. This one is to get everything from a different angle because Jean isn't here. I'll still be using the handheld."

Nicole knew it was too much to ask for. Sandy, along with that extra camera and tripod, went everywhere Lisa and Nicole went. After a while Nicole forgot she was even there. They dressed up for dinners, dressed down to check out the falls, and always wore some sort of pajamas to bed. The week flew by and before they knew it, they were heading home. To Lisa's home. Jean was there waiting with her camera to take over for Sandy.

They were greeted by Lisa's mother, and a very large dog. Very large. Patches of brown-and-black speckled white fur.

"Hey there, boy." Lisa was down on her knees getting a tongue bath from the mutt. "Did he behave himself, Mom?"

"Bruce is always a good boy for me. Aren't ya, fella?" They apparently loved that dog, Bruce, very much. "Hi, Nicole. It's good to see you again. How was your trip?"

"Nice to see you too, Mrs. Morgan. It was very good."

"Let's not be so formal. I'm family now. Call me Betsy," she said.

Lisa stood and took Nicole's hand, pulling her forward. "Nicole. This is Bruce. He's just a big ole baby. Bruce, this is Nicole. You're gonna like her."

Nicole put her free hand out for Bruce to sniff, before running a hand over his massive head. "Hey, big guy."

He let out a *woof* and nuzzled his face into her hand.

"He likes you," Lisa said. "I knew he would."

"Can I get you gals a cup of coffee or anything?" Betsy asked. "I have a pot made."

"No, thank you," Nicole answered.

Lisa declined as well. "Let me show you the house," Lisa said. She led the way, with Bruce following closely behind. The house was modest, boasting two bedrooms, a powder room, and a decent-sized bathroom off the master bedroom. The shower was big enough for two and Nicole wondered how often Lisa had overnight guests that joined her in there. Surprisingly, the thought didn't bring a hint of jealousy.

Lisa's bed was made, but the quilt on one side was wrinkled and in disarray. "Bruce sleeps on that side," Lisa said. "He'll have to start sleeping on the floor. I'll get him a dog bed later today."

Nicole was grateful for that. She wasn't sure there would be enough room on the queen-size bed for the three of them.

"I washed the sheets and the bedspread." Lisa's mom stuck her head in the doorway. "I'm afraid Bruce messed it up again as soon as I made the bed."

"Of course, he did," Lisa responded, giving the dog's head a rub.

"I'm going to get going," Betsy said.

"Thanks for everything." Lisa turned to the dog. "Bruce, tell Grandma good-bye."

Betsy bent to rub the dog's ears. "Good-bye, you big puppy." His butt wiggled like it was on fire. Anything in the vicinity of that tail would have gone flying. Good thing it was short.

Betsy gave each of them a hug and let herself out.

"I'm going to call an Uber to bring me to my apartment so I can get my car and some stuff," Nicole said.

"I can drive you," Lisa responded.

"I appreciate that, but I think Bruce would be upset if you left so soon after getting home." The truth was, Nicole wanted some time alone, away from the attention and cameras. She prayed that Jean wouldn't follow her. "I won't be long."

"Of course. Bring whatever you want. This is your home too. I've already cleaned out several dresser drawers and the second closet in the bedroom is all yours. I'll make room in the bathroom cabinet while you're gone." She paused. "Nicole, I want you to be comfortable here. I know this is a big adjustment."

"It is, but we'll make the best of it. Thank you." She gave Lisa her best reassuring smile. At least she hoped it was reassuring. So many changes all at once was making Nicole's head spin. And not in a good way.

It didn't take long for the Uber to arrive. Lisa gave Nicole a peck on the lips before she headed out the door. That was the extent of their affection except for occasionally holding hands or a random hug. They kept a respectable distance when sleeping at night. Nicole liked Lisa, but so far didn't feel like it was progressing to anything more. She hadn't asked Lisa about her feelings, worried she might be feeling more than Nicole was. Although she gave no indication that that was the case. Jean, thankfully, didn't follow Nicole to her apartment.

Nicole gave Annie a call on the ride. "Hi, Annie. Just wanted to let you know we made it home."

"Great. How did it go?"

"It was good. Lisa's great." She failed to tell Annie that her feelings weren't growing. No need to disappoint her yet. It had only been a little over a week. Still early in their relationship. Maybe it was unrealistic to expect more. Or maybe not, considering she and Lisa had spent just about every moment together since they got married.

"Ready for your *after-the-honeymoon* interview tomorrow?"

"Sure," Nicole said. She wasn't crazy about being interviewed for the camera, but she looked forward to seeing Annie. She'd missed her.

"Nicole, I really appreciate all that you're doing. I know this wasn't part of the plan when you started working for me. I promise to make it up to you."

Nicole had to admit that Annie really was a good person. She wasn't exploiting Nicole, or Lisa for that matter. She was doing everything she could to make things as easy as possible for them. "I appreciate that," Nicole replied.

"I've missed you at work."

"Ditto." The driver pulled into the parking lot of Nicole's apartment building. "Listen, Annie, I just got home—well, to my apartment to get some of my stuff to bring to Lisa's. I'll see you tomorrow."

Annie tossed her phone on the desk. She was surprised how good it was to know Nicole was back from her honeymoon. She had talked to her a few times while she and Lisa were away, but it felt different to know she was so close by. It was more than just needing her at work. But she couldn't quite put her finger on why.

Sandy knocked on her open office door. Annie looked up.

"Hey, boss. I just wanted to upload the footage from the honeymoon."

"Sure. How did it go?"

"It was a pretty low-key trip, but I think I've got some usable stuff." Sandy made her way to the desktop computer in the corner and started the upload.

"Low-key how?"

"Not much action. At least not that I could see."

"What do you mean?" Sometimes getting Sandy to get to the point was like pulling teeth. Well anchored teeth.

"I don't know. They weren't what I would call affectionate. They had some good conversations, but most of it seemed pretty surface. If that makes sense."

It did. Annie wondered what it all meant. They seemed to be getting along, but that could be an illusion. Or maybe they were saving the *good stuff* for when they were alone. Knowing Nicole that was something she might do. She wasn't exactly the *show my innermost thoughts to the world* kind of person. She would find out soon enough when she did the post-honeymoon interview.

"That's gonna take a while." Sandy pointed at the computer. "I'll be back. Need anything? I'm gonna run to Starbucks. Coffee? Something sweet?"

"Speaking of something sweet," Lace said, walking in. "Here I am."

Annie laughed. "Yes, you are." She turned her attention back to Sandy. "No thanks. All set." She held up her insulated oversized travel mug, still filled halfway with coffee. She needed plenty of it to get through the long workdays.

Lace held up a notepad. "I have a list of post-honeymoon questions for you to ask Nicole and Lisa tomorrow. Want to go over them now or should I come back?"

Annie pushed her laptop to the side. "Now."

Lace pulled the chair across from the desk around so she was sitting next to Annie. She smelled like patchouli and lavender. She was obviously born in the wrong decade. "So, we start out light. What was your favorite tourist attraction? How did you like the falls? And then we slowly get into more personal questions. Did you do the nasty?"

Annie snickered. "I hope that's not really in there. At least not like that."

"I was paraphrasing. It's written much more subtle. But as usual, these are just suggestions. By the way, I went through the last of the wedding footage and marked anything interesting." Hiring Lace had been a good decision. She was great at taking initiative and saved Annie so much time. The fact was her whole team was great. The way Nicole stepped up to the plate to save the show was remarkable. Not many people would have done that for her.

They went over the list of questions, eliminating some, adding others, until Annie was satisfied. She wondered if Nicole and Lisa had been *satisfied*—as in intimate. It didn't matter to the show one way or the other. But for some reason it mattered to Annie. There was a part of her that hoped they weren't. Which was totally ridiculous.

Chapter Five

The interview was less than thrilling. There wasn't much for Nicole to share. She tried to make it sound like she'd had the time of her life. "I really like Lisa," she'd told Annie. And she did. Just not the way someone was supposed to like their wife. She felt more like a good friend or even a sister. But Nicole didn't tell Annie that. If her feelings somehow changed, she didn't want it on the record for the world to see that she wasn't feeling the right feelings. Feelings. It was all about the feelings. Or lack thereof. She needed to analyze her computer program to see what questions might be missing to make a better match for future couples. Not that she had given up on the possibility of falling in love with Lisa.

Her first night at Lisa's house felt surreal. This whole experience felt like that. She was married and living in someone else's house with very little prep. If someone had told her six months ago that this was where she would be and what she would be doing, she would have thought they were insane.

Besides not sharing her real feelings with Annie, she didn't share them with Lisa. And Lisa never shared her feelings with Nicole. She got the impression that Lisa liked her but wasn't sure there were feelings beyond that. She wasn't sure how she felt about that. She didn't want Lisa to fall in love with her if she couldn't reciprocate those feelings. But what if she did fall in love with Lisa and Lisa didn't feel the same? Either way there could be a lot of hurt for one of them.

It was good to see Annie, even if it was only for a little while when she was asking questions. She didn't realize how much she'd missed her until she saw her. The extent of it was somewhat of a surprise.

"How's it feel to be back to work?" Annie asked her a couple of days later in Annie's office.

"I am so happy to be back." And she was. "Catch me up?"

"Well, let's see. The first couple seems to be doing good." She smiled. "Sandy and Jean are doing a great job. Jean is following Lisa around today, as you probably know."

"It is so good to get a break from that. I can't say I am thrilled having my life recorded."

"I'm sorry about that. But the success of this show means we get renewed for another season with a bigger budget and a whole new couple. Lace has been a big help with the editing."

"Do I get to see it?" Nicole asked.

"Nope. I'm afraid it will somehow taint your ability to act natural."

"You're afraid I would act unnatural? Maybe supernatural?"

Annie laughed. Nicole warmed to the sound of it. She had been so intent on developing the algorithm and inputting information into the computer that she hadn't really gotten a chance to get to know Annie. She was getting more of a glimpse of who she was, and she was glad about that. She was liking what she saw.

"Yes. I'm afraid you'll start acting supernatural. Like Wonder Woman."

"Would that be a bad thing?"

"I can't afford to get you an invisible plane and I'm not sure what you would do with the lasso of truth."

"Yeah. But having wrist bands that could deflect bullets would be cool."

"Oh my God. I hope you never need anything like that."

Nicole smiled. "Better make me look good on the show so I don't have any enemies in the audience."

Annie tapped her desk. "I don't have to do anything special to make you look good." She got serious for a moment. "Nicole, you are so beautiful and so articulate. You're doing a great job. Not only on the computer, but in this arranged marriage. Everyone is going to love you. Everyone is going to be jealous of Lisa that she gets to be with you and sleep with you every night."

Nicole doubted that. It would probably be Lisa that America fell in love with. If only she could get there herself. True, she hadn't ever expected to do this in the first place. But now that she was in it, she'd had hope that maybe there would be a good ending for them, something she had never believed in before. But the old doubts were creeping back in. Love just wasn't something she was destined for. But she would pretend for a while—for the sake of the show. And for Annie.

"I'm glad you're back," Annie said. "Lunch is on me today. I would love to take you out to a fancy restaurant, but I'm afraid being seen together in public wouldn't be a good idea. The last thing we need is for you to be associated with the show in any way other than being a bride.

"That's understandable. So, you'll order takeout steak and lobster with a bottle of the finest wine?"

Annie laughed again. "If that's what you want."

"How about a cheesesteak sub and a diet soda?"

"You're a cheap date."

"I am. Don't let it get around. It will ruin my reputation. Not that I'll be dating anytime soon, seeing as I'm now married." Nicole held up her hand sporting her wedding ring. It still felt strange on her finger.

Annie felt a sudden urge to intertwine her fingers with the hand Nicole held up. *What the hell?* She'd always thought Nicole was beautiful, but these feelings—whatever they were—were new. And totally inappropriate. Nicole was her employee. Not to mention the fact that she was married. Okay, it was not a marriage that took place because of love, but it looked like it was headed in that direction. Any way you looked at it, it was wrong.

"Where did you just go?" Nicole asked.

"Huh?"

"You looked like you were a million miles away."

"Oh. Yeah. I was just thinking. Nothing important. Cheesesteak and diet soda. That stuff will kill you. You know?"

"I do. But what a way to go. Delicious."

"Okay then. I'll Grubhub it. Now get your ass to work. We need to get going on matching the next couple. I know this show is going to be a hit and we'll be in business for many seasons to come."

"Yes, ma'am." Nicole gave her a mock salute and retreated to her own office.

Annie ordered lunch to be delivered at noon and worked on some boring paperwork until it arrived. She knocked on Nicole's door and held up the bag. "Lunch."

"How high?" Nicole asked.

"What?"

"You say lunch and I ask how high."

Annie laughed. "I believe you ask that when I say *jump.*"

"Oh shit. You're right. I'll remember that when you say jump."

"You're a nut. You know that?"

Nicole pushed her chair back and got up. "I've been told."

"Conference room."

"I thought you had to book that in advance."

Annie put her finger to her lips. "Shh. I won't tell if you won't." Another secret. They seemed to be piling up.

Nicole followed Annie into the conference room and sat down across from her. Annie unbagged their food and slid a beer across the table. "You work hard. I thought you could use a little relaxation. I happened to have these in my mini fridge. Do you drink beer? It's funny. We've worked together for months, but I don't know much about you, other than what I've found out in the interviews for the show. I'd like to remedy that."

"I'd like that. And yes. *Beer would be good.* Really good."

Annie laughed. "I've met your parents and brother of course. You seem like a close family. Has it always been that way?"

Nicole twisted the cap off the bottle. "Yes. I've been very fortunate. My parents have always been very supportive. Even when I came out, they were right there for me. Told me they were proud of me for being true to myself."

"And your brother?" Annie took a bite of her sandwich.

"Same. Even as kids, he stood up for me. There were these bullies on the playground harassing the hell out of me. He took three of them on. Ended up with a black eye but sent them running."

"That's great."

"How about you? What's your family like?" Nicole asked.

Annie shook her head. There hadn't been too many people she shared her childhood story with. She never liked the look of pity in their eyes. But Nicole seemed different somehow. More understanding.

"You don't need to tell me if you don't want to," Nicole said, obviously sensing her discomfort.

"My childhood was pretty sucky to be honest."

"Oh wow. I'm so sorry."

Annie took a long swig of her beer. "My parents are still together, but God only knows why. They fought constantly. Still do. When they got tired of taking it out on each other they took it out on my sister and me."

Nicole reached across the table and placed her hand on top of Annie's. It was warm. Comforting.

"They abused you?" Nicole asked.

"Emotionally. Yes. Not physically. My parents were the total opposite of supportive. If it wasn't for my sister, I wouldn't have had anyone on my side growing up."

"How about friends?"

"I had friends at school of course, but I never brought anyone home. It would have been too embarrassing. I never told them what my home life was like."

"That must have been very lonely." Nicole's eyes held compassion, but not a trace of pity. Annie was glad about that.

"I can't say it was fun."

Nicole retrieved her hand to unwrap her sandwich. Annie missed the comfort of it. "And now? With your parents?"

"I mostly avoid them. They told me how stupid I was for leaving my job to start this production company."

"That's awful," Nicole said.

"The funny thing is they love reality TV. But they hate the idea of this show because it's queer. They have never met anyone I've dated. Not that I would want them to."

"Are you dating anyone, now?" Nicole asked. "I mean, you've never mentioned anyone."

"No. Not in a long while. My career has become my lover. Hard to cuddle up to it at night, though." She laughed. A sad laugh.

Nicole felt bad for her, but also somehow relieved that she didn't have a girlfriend. Weird.

"I can understand that. I gave up on love a long time ago. And here I am married. So hey, anything can happen." Nicole took a bite of her food. A drip of steak sauce escaped and dribbled down her chin. Annie reached over with a napkin, and for a moment, Nicole thought she was going to wipe it for her. But she handed her the napkin instead. "Thanks."

"You're married because we were in a bind. I hope you didn't feel like you were forced to do it."

"I did it willingly. And it's not horrible."

Annie laughed. "Not horrible is good. Right? I would have hoped for more than *not horrible*."

"I wasn't sure what to hope for. After I met—no—actually, after I *saw* Lisa, I thought maybe something good coming out of this was possible. You have to admit she's beautiful."

"Of course."

"Anyway, it kicked up something in me that I thought was dead." At least in that moment it did. Lust. It seemed to be fading the more she got to know Lisa. Nicole still found her beautiful—but more like a beautiful friend than a lover.

"That's a good thing, right? It kicking up and all?"

"Sure. Always good to rediscover parts of yourself that you thought were dead." Even if the person who kicked it up probably wasn't the one for you.

"Then I'm glad I let you do it."

"Actually, I am too." Even if she didn't fall in love with Lisa at least she knew it was still a possibility somewhere. Some day. She was okay with that. "You said you have a sister," Nicole said, changing the subject.

"Yes. Terry. Two years older than me. Sort of like your brother. Except the bullies she protected me from were our parents. How crappy is that? She looked out for me. Took the brunt of the abuse whenever she could to save me from it. She believed in me. Supported me in this endeavor. I'm not sure where I would be without her." She wiped a tear that trickled down her cheek. "She's married to a wonderful guy. Dean."

Nicole felt her own eyes welling up. "I'm so glad you have her. And if it means anything to you, I'm here for you too. I believe in you."

"That means more than I can say. Thank you, Nicole."

Annie hugged her before they both went back to work. Nicole figured the extra tight squeeze at the end was to let her know how much her support meant to Annie. She was glad if she was making a difference in Annie's life. She'd had no idea how hard her life had been. She made a mental note to make sure she told Annie more often that she appreciated her.

She had just started putting data about the newest bride candidates into her computer when she got a text from her mother. *Dinner on Sunday at 6 bring Lisa*

Nicole smiled. Her mother's texts were often short and right to the point. She wasn't crazy about using a cell phone. They still had a landline mounted on the wall, although they rarely used it.

Nicole sent a quick text to Lisa. *My mother invited us for dinner Sunday. Are you game?*

Sure. Lisa responded. *I'm up for anything that doesn't involve me cooking.*

Nicole felt a pang of guilt. Lisa had done most of the cooking since they returned from their honeymoon. Nicole had assumed she liked it and offered because she was off work for the summer. She'd have to make up for that.

We'll be there. Nicole responded to her mother. She got three purple emoji hearts back.

Nicole pulled the next application from the stack. Forty-three-year-old lesbian, originally from Boston now living in Delaware. They were categorizing everyone by age and state. She opened the folder on her computer for forty-year-olds, and entered the information. The idea was to have brides from different decades for each season. Each season would consist of sixteen episodes, lasting approximately four months each, with two seasons planned for each year with a four-month gap between them. But future seasons depended on the success of this one. The weight of it felt heavy on Nicole's shoulders. She continued entering the data as if her career depended on it. Because it did.

Chapter Six

What can I do to help?" Nicole asked her mother. Jean had accompanied them with the camera.

"You can go help your father in the garage," she said. "Lisa can keep me company." She turned to Lisa. "Is that okay?"

"Sure," Lisa said. She smiled at Nicole. "I'll be fine. I'm sure the stories about your mother have been exaggerated."

"She's a funny one," her mother said. "I like her." She gently pushed Nicole toward the back door. "Go. Your father needs help."

Jean looked torn for a moment, not sure which one of them to follow. She decided to stay with Lisa and Nicole's mom.

Nicole glanced back at Lisa and shrugged before heading out the door to the detached garage. "Hey, Dad. Mom said you need help." He was leaning over some engine parts on his work bench.

He looked up. "She did, did she?"

"She did."

"Then I guess you better help me. But I'll be damned if I know what I need help with."

"That's kind of what I thought. Why did she want to ambush Lisa?"

Her dad wiped some grease from his hands onto a rag that didn't look like it could hold much more dirt. How something that filthy could help clean his hands was anybody's guess. "I wouldn't exactly call it an ambush. More like a friendly conversation. To tell you the truth she wants to welcome her to the family."

"If that's all it is, why did she feel the need to kick me out?"

"You know your mom. There is nothing to worry about."

There was a knock on the opened garage door. Nicole turned as Marley and Ted walked in. "Mom said you need our help," Ted said. He scrunched up his face. "You don't really, do you?"

"Of course, I do. Your mother doesn't lie. I need—um—a new rag." He held the dirty one up. "There's some in the top drawer of my toolbox."

"And that takes three of us?" Ted asked.

"I need three of them."

"She wanted alone time with Lisa," Nicole said.

"I figured," Ted said.

"Hey," Marley piped up. "She did the same thing with me after Ted and I got engaged."

"She did?" Ted asked.

"Yeah. Remember? I told you she sat me down, looked me right in the eyes and had me shaking in my boots. I didn't know what the heck she was going to do or say. I didn't know her too well at that point."

"Oh, I do remember now," Ted said.

"Well?" Nicole asked. "What did she say to you?"

Marley laughed. "She welcomed me to the family. Said she considered me one of her kids and that she would always be there for me. I imagine she's doing the same with Lisa."

Nicole had never known her mother to be mean to anyone but was still relieved with Marley's revelation. "How long do you think this is going to take?"

Her dad glanced at his watch. "She should be just about done. I think it's safe to return to the house." Ted, Marley, and

Nicole filed out. "Hey," he called after them. "No one got me a clean rag."

"I really like your family," Lisa said on the ride home. "And your mom is a great cook." Dinner had been very nice. Relaxing.

Nicole took her hand, keeping her other hand firmly on the steering wheel. "They are pretty great. And speaking of cooking, I promise to help out more with that."

"What?"

"With the cooking. I realized I haven't been a very good wife in that department."

"You work all day. I don't expect you to come home and make dinner."

"Then how about I make dinner on the weekends. Or better yet, take you out to dinner."

"I would like that." Lisa smiled. If Nicole was going to make this work, and she really did want to try, she knew she would have to be all in. Not that she hadn't been up to that point, but perhaps upping her game was called for. Maybe then the correct feelings would come.

Bruce greeted them at the door, doing his happy dance and just about knocking Nicole over with his massive butt. She scooted around him and let Lisa take the brunt of his affection. It wasn't that she didn't like him—or dogs in general. It was just that he was Lisa's dog. Just like this was Lisa's house. And Lisa's dishes. And Lisa's bed. And Lisa's everything. She missed her own apartment, her own stuff. Between work and her everyday life, she hadn't really had a chance to go home and just be. She missed that. Oh, well. This was life now. She needed to just accept that. And for the most part, she believed she did.

"Come here," she said to Lisa once Bruce had calmed down. She wrapped her arms around Lisa's waist, well aware that Jean was right there catching every detail. She placed a small kiss on her lips and then pulled her in closer for a much longer, more intimate kiss. Lisa's lips parted and welcomed Nicole's tongue in. Lisa deepened the kiss. And Nicole felt... What? Nothing? She felt nothing. The chemistry just wasn't there for her. Instead of getting lost in the moment she was totally in her head, trying to figure out how to get out of the kiss without hurting Lisa's feelings or letting it progress any further.

It was Lisa who pulled away first. Nicole was grateful and wondered if she'd had the same reaction.

❖

Annie moved to the desk in the corner and pulled up some of the recent footage Lace had marked as usable. Her stomach dropped when she watched the scene in Lisa's living room with Nicole and Lisa kissing. She was sure it was what the viewers would want to see, but it made her uncomfortable. Their relationship seemed to be progressing.

Maybe a little drama would make for better ratings. Was there an ethical way to stir the pot—cause a little discord? There was a part of Annie that knew it wasn't a nice thing to do. But the business side of her, the one that needed this show to succeed, knew it would be important to have conflict—something that had been lacking up until now.

She rolled her office chair to the door, opened it, and called down the hall to Lace. Sometimes that was easier than using her phone.

"What can I do you for?" Lace asked thirty seconds later. Her pink hair was flopping over as she tilted her head to one side.

"Let's go have a little meeting at the coffee shop next door." Nicole was working in her office just down the hall, and Annie didn't want to be overheard.

"Sure. But I can run and get you coffee if you want."

"No. I would rather take a walk." Annie tilted her head in the direction of Nicole's office and winked. She hoped Lace would get her silent message.

"Sounds good to me. I could use some coffee. And a walk."

The coffee shop was relatively empty considering it was between the breakfast and lunch rush. Annie was grateful for that. She paid for two cups of coffee and a couple of bagels, and they made their way to the farthest table away from the few people in the place.

"So, what's going on, boss, that you don't want Nicole to hear?"

Annie took her time explaining, choosing her words carefully. "Don't judge me," she said after she explained.

"I do judge you. I judge you are an exceptional producer, and you are going to have an awesome show. Now, what kind of conflict?" Lace asked.

"I'm not sure. That's what I wanted to talk to you about. Thought we could brainstorm."

"The idea is to cause an argument. Right? Maybe cause some jealousy."

"That might do it. They seem to get along good over everything else. Nicole didn't even put up a fuss over leaving her apartment to move into Lisa's house. Even that huge ass dog doesn't seem to bother her, and I've seen footage of him jumping up on the bed with them. I like dogs and all, but I would have pitched a bitch if I had been her."

"Okay, so Nicole is pretty easygoing. What have you observed about Lisa? What do you think would set her off?"

"We could steal her dog."

"Ha ha. I'm thinking no. We want to cause conflict, not panic. And that wouldn't start a fight between her and Nicole. I think Nicole would step up and do everything she could to find him."

"I was just kidding. Going back to the jealousy thing. Would it be better to make Nicole jealous or Lisa?" Lace sipped her coffee. "Damn. That's hot."

Annie moved the bowl with mini creamers in her direction. "I think it would be better to make Lisa jealous. Nicole didn't want to do this in the first place. Lisa has been all in since the beginning."

"That's right. How do we do this? We're going to need someone to show interest in Nicole. Who could we get to do that? It needs to be someone we can trust." She poured three creamers into her coffee and stacked the empty containers on top of each other. "Should we let Nicole in on the plan?"

"Absolutely not. The fight needs to be real, even if the reason behind it isn't."

"Gotcha."

"I'll do it," Annie said.

"Do what?"

Annie couldn't help but roll her eyes. "Try to keep up with the conversation here. I'll show interest in Nicole. Flirt with her in front of Lisa."

"Won't that cause a problem between you and Lisa?"

"I hadn't thought of that. Hmm. It definitely could." Think. "What else can we do?"

"I still think jealousy is the best bet. We just need someone to do it. I don't think she would buy it if it was me. Being straight and all."

"Right. Maybe Jean or Sandy?"

"Sandy might work. Jean is married. Her wife might not like this little game if she got wind of it."

Game. Is that all this was? Just one big game? No. It was much more than that. It was her career. And Nicole's for that matter. "Do you think Sandy would do it? I mean, it would make sense. She's spent lots of time with them. It's conceivable she could develop feelings. Lisa would believe it." Annie paused. "But is it enough? I mean if Sandy makes moves and Nicole doesn't respond to her, which I'm sure she wouldn't, would that upset Lisa enough to start a fight?"

"Probably not. We need to plant something that makes Lisa think Nicole has a wandering eye."

"It can't be anything that they can't come back from. Something that can be explained away eventually as a misunderstanding," Annie said.

"Yes!" Lace exclaimed.

"So?"

"I don't know. But we are heading in the right direction."

"We need to make Lisa think something is going on that isn't."

"Something on Nicole's phone. A picture maybe. Or an email from someone."

Annie shook her head. "I don't think Lisa would be looking at Nicole's phone. Maybe a love note left where she could see it."

"That might work. It would be easy enough to slip it into the house. Sandy and Jean are there all the time. And you too from time to time."

"True. Why don't you work on something that will set the ball in motion. Let me know when you have it. We'll give them another couple of weeks of wedded bliss and then we'll plant it." The guilt Annie was feeling was mixed with—what? She didn't know.

It had been a few weeks since they'd had dinner with Nicole's family. She and Lisa seemed to be settling into a comfortable routine, getting to know each other and learning what to expect.

"What is this?" Lisa asked Nicole.

Nicole took the piece of paper from her, keenly aware of Sandy being close by with the camera focused on her. Jean was farther back in the room, taking in the whole scene, Nicole assumed. She read what was written on it silently.

Nicole,

I had so much fun on our date. I look forward to next time.

XOXO

Me

"I have no idea. Where did you find it?"

"On the floor in front of your nightstand."

Nicole knew without a doubt it had been planted to cause trouble—an unexpected plot twist for the show. It was all about those damn ratings. Of course, those damn ratings meant her working on the show for years to come or her applying for unemployment after this season. A million thoughts went through her mind at once. This was expected to cause a fight. She was sure of it. If Lisa didn't push it, should she? She was more than a little pissed at Annie for putting her in this position. Sandy in her peripheral vision was pointing at the note with her free hand and nodding, balancing the camera on her shoulder.

Nicole shook her head. What the hell? She was expected to read it out loud for the cameras. She wasn't liking this game. She handed it back to Lisa and nodded at her as soon as Sandy moved the camera from her to Lisa.

Lisa looked at her with a question in her eyes.

Read it out loud, Nicole mouthed. If ratings were what they were after, it made more sense this way.

A look of understanding registered on Lisa's face. Nicole wondered how Annie could have thought that either one of them were so stupid that they wouldn't be able to figure out what she was doing. They were smart enough to know what she wanted, and Nicole decided to go along with it. She hoped Lisa would do the same. It would have been nice if Annie had trusted Nicole enough to let her in on the plan.

Lisa didn't disappoint. She read the note out loud. "Nicole, who is this from? Being married means you aren't supposed to be dating anyone. But obviously you didn't get the memo." She had the appropriate amount of anger and disappointment in her voice. She would have been a great actress.

"That must be an old note. I haven't been seeing anyone."

"You expect me to believe that? Why would an old note suddenly show up on the floor?"

Jean had moved in closer, so she didn't miss a moment of the fake tense action.

"Baby, you've got to believe me." That may have been a little over the top.

"You can just sleep on the couch until you decide to tell me the truth," Lisa spit out. She made a show of crumpling up the note and throwing it toward Nicole's face. Nicole caught it in midair. Four years of softball paid off. Lisa turned and stomped off in the direction of the bedroom, only to return a minute later with a pillow and blanket, which she dumped at Nicole's feet.

"What the hell?" Nicole said.

"What the hell?" Lisa responded and disappeared into the bedroom again. It was an Academy Award-winning performance.

Nicole kicked the pile at her feet, grabbed her keys and phone from the table by the door, and left the house, slamming the door behind her.

She half expected Sandy or Jean to follow her. They didn't. She drove directly to the office. Just as she suspected, Annie was still there working. She didn't bother knocking. "What the hell?" she said. It seemed to be the catchphrase of the evening.

CHAPTER SEVEN

Annie looked up from her laptop. "The note?"

"The note." Nicole pulled the chair from the corner up to the desk and plopped down. "A heads-up would have been nice."

"I'm sorry." She seemed sincere. "I thought it would be a more realistic reaction if it was unexpected. You understand why I did it. Right?"

"I do. Lisa and I gave your cameras quite the performance."

"Was Lisa really mad?"

Nicole shook her head. "Lisa is not stupid. She knew it was planted. We *acted* for the cameras."

Annie looked disappointed.

"Were you hoping she bought it for real and was jealous? You wanted her to get mad at me? That's really messed up, Annie."

"I don't know what I was hoping for, except for a little conflict for the audience. You two seem to be getting along too well."

"I thought you wanted us to be ourselves. Now we're in trouble for liking each other?"

Annie pulled the dark-rimmed glasses from the top of her head down and slipped them on her face. Nicole couldn't help but notice that it raised her hot factor up a few notches. "Of course, I want you to be yourself. I truly am sorry if it made you feel uncomfortable."

"Wasn't that the whole point? To put us on the spot and make us react?"

Annie was silent. Yes. That was the point. But she never intended to hurt Nicole in the process. That was the last thing she wanted to do. She truly cared about her. Not only as an employee, but also as a friend. Maybe more than a friend. No. Not more than a friend. She could never be more than a friend. If she truly cared, wouldn't she want Nicole to be happy? Happy with Lisa? Which she seemed to be. It was too confusing to try to sort out. She needed to keep her head in the game, and the game was producing a top-rated TV show. That was all. That was why she had Sandy plant the note. She had nothing to apologize for. She wasn't the only one who would win if this was a hit. Nicole would too. Maybe in more ways than one. She might find love. It seemed to be heading in that direction.

"Well?" Nicole's eyes bored into her as she waited for an answer.

"Yes. Is that what you want to hear? I wanted you and Lisa to react. To play a part for the camera. To get the audience interested and invested in your relationship." Her words sounded harsh, and in the moment she didn't care. She was doing this as much for Nicole as she was for herself. If Nicole couldn't see that, then that was her problem.

Nicole seemed at a loss for words. She got her answer. She got the truth. But Annie wasn't sure she knew what to do with it.

"I'm not the enemy, Nicole," Annie said, much more softly. "I want this to work for all of us."

"I felt blindsided. I didn't like it."

"I can understand that. Maybe you and Lisa can come up with some—I don't know—juicy stuff on your own. Talk about it when the cameras are off. In the bedroom at night." Annie didn't want to think about what else might be going on in the bedroom at night. *Stop. It. Now.*

"So, you want us to start making stuff up?"

"No. Not exactly. We need to keep the show authentic. But maybe any disagreements or squabbles can be exaggerated for the cameras."

"And if we don't have any disagreements or squabbles?"

"I find it hard to believe that in four months you are going to agree on everything. Isn't there anything that you find annoying about Lisa?" Annie put her hand up. "Wait. Don't answer that. It's one of the questions for the next interview."

"We're supposed to tell the whole world what we don't like about each other?"

Annie found herself getting annoyed all over again. "Yes, Nicole. That is the point of the show. You get married. You may or may not fall in love. You tell the world what the journey is like. At the end you decide if you want to stay married or end it in divorce. And the world gets to watch. You have known all along what the show was about."

"Yes, but I didn't know what it would be like to be under the microscope all the time. When I took this job I thought I would be quietly in the background, at my desk, in front of the computer—alone. Sans cameras and an audience."

She had a point. She had stepped up to save the show. She didn't deserve what Annie was pushing on her. But there was no other way. Was there? The simple answer was no. The show needed drama. Conflict. But Annie didn't have to be so harsh. "You're right. It wasn't the original plan. I'm open to ideas to make this work. I will have to ask some hard, personal questions. You're always free to answer them however you see fit. I won't push. It's the best I can do. How does that sound?"

Nicole nodded. "I guess I can live with that. I'll talk to Lisa when we're alone about spicing things up. But I need to keep things honest. Well, as honest as I can be considering I'm lying by omission to my wife about my job and my connection with this show."

"It's not forever. You can tell her at the end of the four months. Until then, I'm sorry. It's not a possibility."

"I know that. I don't plan on telling her now."

"On another note," Annie said, trying to change the subject. "The network wants to run the pilot next month."

"What? How is that even possible? We still have almost three months to go. Networks don't rush this kind of thing."

"They want to spark interest for the October release. The wedding and honeymoon footage is all we need for the pilot. Lace and I have been working overtime to get it edited. We got this. It will help us in the long run. Are you still on board? I need to know for sure."

"Yes. I told you I would do this. And I'll follow through."

"Nicole, please don't be mad at me." It was a lame thing to say. Annie didn't know why it was so important, but she didn't want any bad blood between them.

Nicole tapped her finger on Annie's desk. "Don't pull any more surprises and we'll be just fine."

"Okay." It was all Annie could manage to say. She was used to being in control. To calling all the shots. But she was backing down from this one. Giving Nicole her way.

Nicole nodded. "Okay. I'm going to get home—to Lisa's house. I have a couch to make up. Thanks to your little game, I've been kicked out of the bedroom."

Annie couldn't help but laugh. She quickly put her hand over her mouth. "Sorry. I guess my plan worked. You could always spend the night with me. At my place. In the guest room," she added quickly. "It's got a nice comfortable bed."

"Not going home after a fight—even if it was fake—would be good for the show. Right?"

Annie put up her hands. "Honestly, that's not what I was thinking. I was just trying to make your night easier for you. You do whatever you think is right."

"Besides, I have my own apartment if I didn't want to go back to Lisa's. But that's where I'm going. I'm sure Lisa will let me back into the bedroom as soon as Sandy and or Jean, whoever is still there, leaves for the night. I guess if I'm still in bed when they get there in the morning, we'll just pretend we made up."

"Good plan. I'm going to head home too. It's been a long day. Too long. I'll walk out with you."

She saved the work on her laptop and closed it. She was tempted to take it home but knew she would be up half the night working if she did. She needed to get a good night's sleep for once.

Her plan sounded good in theory, but she spent most of the night tossing and turning, replaying the conversation with Nicole on a continuous loop in her head. Had she done the right thing, having Sandy plant the note? She had to admit that there was an edge of cruelty to it. And she wasn't an evil person. And she didn't ever want Nicole to think she was.

❖

Just as Nicole had predicted, Lisa came out of the bedroom as soon as the cameras left. "You don't really need to sleep on the couch. I assumed you wanted me to have a fit over that fake note."

"I did. It was a shitty little trick that Annie pulled to try to make things more interesting for the audience. I told her exactly what I thought of it."

Lisa pushed the blanket to the side and sat on the couch next to Nicole. "Does she think we're too boring for TV?"

"She said we were getting along too well." Nicole shook her head. "We do get along well, but…" She let her words trail off, not sure how to phrase what she wanted to say.

"But what?"

"We haven't really talked about how we're really feeling. About each other."

"No, we haven't. We sort of started in the middle. We became an old married couple without one single date."

"I know you went into this hoping for forever. Do you still think that's a possibility?"

"To be honest, it's too early to tell. I like you. I know that much. We *do* get along well." Lisa let out a small laugh. "Too good, according to Annie. But I barely know you. I would like to say yes, we are heading to forever, but there is no way to know at this point."

Nicole didn't want to dash Lisa's hopes. She didn't want to tell her she felt more like a sister than a lover. Hell, she felt more when Annie hugged her than when Lisa hugged her. Wait. What? What *did* she feel when Annie hugged her? She felt warm. Tingly. That didn't make sense. Annie had only hugged her a few times. Why did she feel anything? Annie was her boss. That's all. That's all she could ever be.

"How do you feel?" Lisa's question interrupted her thoughts.

"Huh? Oh. Pretty much the same."

"So, we keep going? Get to know each other? See where it leads?"

"That sounds like a plan," Nicole answered.

Lisa rose and put her hand out to Nicole. Nicole took it and let Lisa pull her up and lead her to the bedroom. Lisa curled up against Nicole in bed with her head on Nicole's shoulder and Nicole's arm wrapped around Lisa's waist, her hand resting on Lisa's stomach. It was the first time they'd been this close in bed.

It felt strange. Unnatural. Forced. Nicole wondered if she was the only one feeling that way.

Nicole wasn't sure when it happened, but when she woke up in the morning, Lisa had retreated to her own side. Nicole was glad she didn't have to untangle from her before slipping out of bed.

She was pouring coffee into her travel mug when Lisa emerged, still wearing her night shirt, from the bedroom. She sat at the table. Nicole poured her a cup of coffee, added milk and just a bit of sugar. She set it down in front of her.

"You're an angel," Lisa said. "I'm half tempted to ask you to marry me. I could get used to this service."

"I'm sorry," Nicole said. "I'm taken." She held up her hand, wiggling her ring finger.

"Damn. Always the bridesmaid."

Nicole kissed her on the top of her head. "Gotta go. I'll see you after work."

"Bye, babe. Have a good day."

The endearment didn't escape Nicole's notice. She couldn't quite return it. "Bye, Lisa." She wasn't sure if she ever could.

The traffic was lighter than usual, and she got to the office in record time. She grabbed her coffee and headed into the building and up to the third floor. She took the stairs instead of the elevator as she sometimes did. Formal exercise wasn't her thing, but she tried to get extra walking or climbing in whenever she could. Computer work equaled a whole lot of sitting.

There was a yellow Post-it Note on Nicole's office door. *Please come to my office when you get here.—Annie*

What now? Nicole always hated it when her mother said things like *I need to talk to you.* Don't announce it. Just talk to me. It always left an uneasy feeling in her stomach.

She did an about-face and knocked on Annie's door. "Come in."

Nicole opened the door and stuck her head in. "You summoned?"

"I did. Come on in and shut the door."

Being told to shut the door did nothing to calm the churning of her insides. She did as she was told and sat across from Annie.

Annie closed her laptop and ran a hand through her hair. From the looks of it, she had done that several times already that morning.

Nicole tilted her head and raised her eyebrows, hoping Annie would just start talking. Several long beats went by before she did.

"Nicole, I want to apologize again. I'm so sorry about that stupid note. I never meant to cause you any stress."

Nicole wasn't sure what to expect, but this wasn't it. She breathed a sigh of relief. "Okay. I accept your apology."

"Are we good? I don't want any bad feelings between us."

"Annie, we're fine. No worries. We went through this already."

"I know we have. But it's really been bothering me. I hardly slept last night thinking about it."

"I'm sorry about that."

Annie laughed. "I screw up and you're the one saying sorry. That's just like you, Nicole. That's why I think so much of you. You are the real deal. A truly good person."

"Um, thanks. I'm not sure what to say."

"Just say you forgive me," Annie said.

"*I do*. Wait. Saying that is what got me into trouble in the first place. Let me rephrase. I forgive you."

"I hope you don't think of your marriage as trouble."

"No. Not really trouble. Just different."

"I can understand that. I would thank you again for doing this, but I think the first five hundred times I said it got the point across."

"Aww. I'm disappointed that I'm not going to get thanked five hundred and one times, but I guess I can live with that."

"I really do appreciate it."

"Okay. Close enough."

"How are you doing with the new applications?"

"To be honest, they all tend to blend together. It does seem like there are more women in their forties that have applied. The first round had a lot of women in their twenties."

"That's good. We don't want to go too young. I think older women know what they want more. Once the show hits the air we are going to have women coming out of the woodwork wanting to get married."

"Sounds creepy."

Annie laughed. "Not like mice. Like we will have tons of women to choose from. It's going to be good, Nicole. We can do this. Conquer the world of reality TV, baby. You and me."

That was the last thing Nicole wanted. She just wanted to sit behind her computer, create algorithms and input data. Nice and quiet. No cameras. No one recording her every move.

"Lunch today?"

"That would be great," Nicole said. She enjoyed spending time with Annie apart from their regular work.

"What would you like? Computer programmer's choice today."

Nicole laughed. "How do you feel about Chinese food?"

"Love it."

"Great. Whatever you get will be fine. There's not much I don't like."

"Chopsticks?" Annie asked.

"Of course. I'm not an animal."

"Good to know. Chopsticks it is. I'll let you know when it gets here."

Nicole was ready for a break by the time Annie knocked on her opened door.

"Lunch," Annie said, holding up a couple of paper bags. "The conference room is in use, so sneaking in there isn't a possibility today. It's a beautiful day. How about we go to the park?" The park behind their office building was rarely busy on weekdays.

"Perfect. Let me just..." Nicole saved her latest entry and stood.

Annie was right. It was a beautiful day, not as hot as most August days in central New York could be.

There were several unoccupied picnic tables scattered throughout the small park. Annie led them to one under the shade of a large oak tree. The only other person around was a young guy pitching a ball to a little white dog who eagerly chased it and brought it back to him. Again and again.

"You are looking great. Marriage must agree with you," Annie said.

It doesn't feel like a marriage, Nicole thought. More like sleeping with a roommate. "Thanks," she said, not sharing her feelings.

Sunlight filtered through the leaves as the light breeze swayed the branches. It bounced off Annie's dark hair giving it a soft glow. A sexy glow. Nicole blinked the thought away. Without her permission, her eyes traveled to Annie's lips. Full lips. Kissable lips. What the actual hell? Why was her brain going to unacceptable places? Or maybe it was her libido. Good to know it wasn't dead. With her sisterly feelings and lack of sexual attraction to Lisa, despite her beauty, Nicole had thought maybe it was. But aiming these feelings at Annie was just wrong.

Annie noticed Nicole's eyes glaze over for a moment, right after looking at Annie's lips. And then subtly licking her own. At least that's what Annie thought she had been looking at. Given a different set of circumstances she might have leaned across the table and kissed her. She wanted to. Wanted to kiss a married woman. A woman who seemed happy in her marriage. But happy or not, Nicole was off limits.

"Whatcha got in here?" Nicole asked, peering into the bag.

Annie was glad for the sudden distraction. "You wanted Chinese. I got Chinese." She told Nicole what was in each container as she retrieved it from the bag. She retrieved two bottles of beer from the smaller bag.

"Perfect," Nicole said.

Annie smiled. Sometimes a beer when she was working late would help her get through the evening. Sharing one with Nicole was much better.

Nicole twisted off the cap and held her bottle up. "To you and your magic mini fridge."

Annie opened her bottle and clinked it against Nicole's. "Cheers. Oh, yeah..." She reached into the large bag one more time. "Chopsticks." She handed a set to Nicole. "I have a confession to make." She let several long beats go by.

"Do you want to tell me, or should I call a priest?"

Annie laughed. "No priest necessary. My confession—well—I've never used chopsticks before. I'm not sure how to do it."

Nicole's smile lit up her face. "You're in luck then. Because I'm an expert." She unwrapped her chopsticks, pulled them apart, and motioned for Annie to do the same. "One stick stays stationary. It never moves. Hold the bottom part between your middle and ring finger and the upper part rest between your thumb and pointer finger. Like this." She demonstrated.

"Like this?" Annie asked, imitating the way Nicole held it.

"Perfect. Now hold the other one with your thumb and pointer. Move it up and down to grasp the food."

Annie watched Nicole do it and tried to do what she did but couldn't get the chopsticks to close properly. The piece of chicken she tried to pick up slipped between them and flew halfway across the table.

"Watch again," Nicole said. Without missing a beat, she picked up the piece of chicken Annie had lost control of with her chopsticks and dropped it on the ground behind her. "One for the squirrels," she said. "One more time. This stick stays in place and this one..." She wiggled the top chopstick. "And this one moves. Give it another try."

Annie tried to mirror her moves but couldn't pick anything up no matter how hard she tried.

"Oh man. I know what the problem is. You're left-handed and these are right-handed chopsticks."

"Oh." Annie examined the chopsticks in her hand. Nicole burst out laughing. "What?"

"They're just straight sticks. There aren't any left or right ones."

Annie shook her head. "You're very funny. I fell for it. I was trying to figure out what the difference would be."

"Actually, I think the problem is your sticks aren't even the way you're holding them. Make sure you line up the bottom, so they're the same length."

Annie adjusted them and gave it another try. Still no luck. Embarrassment was creeping in.

Nicole moved to the other side of the table and sat next to Annie straddling the bench. She adjusted the chopsticks in Annie's hand, placed her hand over Annie's, and moved Annie's fingers with hers. Annie sucked in a breath as a tingle from Nicole's touch ran up her arm and made her heart beat a little faster. Together they picked up a piece of chicken and Nicole held on as she guided it to Annie's mouth. Annie dipped her head, retrieved the piece, and slowly chewed it.

"Think you got it now?" Nicole asked.

Annie was tempted to say no, so Nicole wouldn't retreat to the other side of the table again. But she didn't want to seem obvious. "I, um…yeah. I think so."

"Give it a try." Nicole let go of her hand.

Annie was able to get another piece of chicken to her mouth.

"There. You've got it." Nicole grabbed the container of lo mein and expertly scooped some up and into her mouth. She stayed planted next to Annie.

"Damn, you're good at that," Annie said, watching her chew. "Can you do it with the fried rice?" No way could anyone pick up something that small with chopsticks.

"Sure. With the rice it's more like scooping." She demonstrated.

"I'm very impressed," Annie said. She reached once more into the bag and pulled out a plastic fork. "And I appreciate the lesson. But I'll either starve to death or be here till midnight if I continue with the chopsticks."

"Understood. You do you."

Annie thought of a very inappropriate response about *doing* Nicole but decided against saying it out loud.

They ate in silence for several minutes. "Thank you for this," Nicole said, breaking the quiet. "I've had a hankering for a while."

"Hankering?"

Nicole smiled. "It's something my dad always says."

"I like it. I think I'll use it. I'm glad I could satisfy your hankering."

"It's good to have my hankering satisfied."

"I had a hankering to—" Annie stopped. She almost said she had a hankering to satisfy Nicole. She started again. "A hankering to learn to eat with chopsticks. I'm going to practice, and you will be uber impressed next time."

"I'll add it to my list of things that impresses me about you."

Annie laughed. "Oh yeah. What else is on that list?"

"Oh no. I'm not going to tell you. You'll get a swollen head and then you'll be impossible to live with."

"Okay, then. I'll just have to use my imagination."

"Speaking of imagination, I've never asked you whatever gave you the idea of having two strangers get married and creating a reality show out of it? Are you a true romantic at heart?"

"Do I strike you as a romantic?" Annie asked. She'd never thought of herself that way. But maybe with the right person, she could be.

Nicole tilted her head and seemed to examine her. She scrunched up her face and nodded. "I can see some romance, hidden in there. Somewhere safe, where the spiders and the rust can't get at it."

Annie hadn't expected that answer.

"Well?" Nicole raised her eyebrows, waiting for an answer.

"Maybe. Somewhere deep down. The short answer is I've seen so many relationships fail because they were started for the wrong reasons. I thought if two people were matched by experts—by data—your data, then there might be a chance. I know it won't work a hundred percent of the time, but I hoped it would work often enough."

"I like that answer. Why turn it into a reality show?"

"I've always loved reality shows and who doesn't like a good love story?"

"See. I knew there was romance in there somewhere." Nicole's smile traveled from her lips to her eyes, and they lit up. For a long moment Annie couldn't look away.

"Maybe," she finally said. "Maybe."

CHAPTER EIGHT

Another three weeks went by in a blur. Nicole was settling into Lisa's house, getting used to having Bruce around—he insisted on sleeping on her feet at night—and not being in her own space. Her feelings for Lisa hadn't changed and at this rate, Nicole was pretty sure they weren't going to.

She was nearly to work when her phone rang. She knew it was Marley from the ringtone, "Best Friend" by Brandy. She liked knowing who was calling before she answered her phone. Lisa's ringtone was "Going to the Chapel" by the Crystals and Annie's was "She Works Hard for the Money" by Donna Summer. She chose each ringtone carefully. "Hey, Marley."

"Happy birthday, girlfriend."

"Thanks."

"What special plans do you have for today?"

"No plans. Going to work. Heading home. I imagine Lisa will have dinner ready."

"Is she at least making you something special?"

"Not that I know of. I don't think she remembered it's my birthday."

"What? You didn't drop any hints? I'm going to call her and remind her."

Nicole pulled into the parking lot. "No. Don't. Please. It's no big deal. Really."

"How about I stop by your office at lunch time and drop off a piece of cake at least?"

Nicole felt a moment of panic. No one was supposed to know that she worked on *I Do, I Don't*. She hadn't shared exactly what she was doing when she got the job. As far as Marley and the rest of her family knew, she was just doing computer programming. There was something she had found a little degrading about working on a reality show. She never expected to actually *be* the reality show. "Today's not good," Nicole told her. "Maybe we can get together for dinner one night this week."

"That sounds good. Just you and me, or are we inviting the balls and chains?"

Nicole laughed. "Your choice. I don't think Lisa would mind if I went out without her if that's what you prefer."

"You *don't think*? Haven't you been out without her since you've been married?"

Nicole had to take a second to think. "No. I don't believe I have."

"Wow. You really are tied down."

"No. That's not it. We're just taking our time to get to know each other."

"And how is that going?" Marley asked.

"How about we catch up over that dinner. I just got to work, so I need to go in."

"Sure. Go ahead. Happy birthday again. I love ya."

"Thanks. Love you, too. Bye, Marley."

Her phone pinged with several messages as she took the elevator to the third floor. Some days the stairs seemed like a mountain she didn't want to climb. She waited until she was in her office before she looked at the texts. Her brother, mother, and father all sent her birthday wishes. Her mother's text said she would call her after work. A couple more texts from friends came later that day. She was surprised when a text from

Annie popped in. She hadn't mentioned it was her birthday. Not that it was a secret, but Nicole had never been one to shout it out or seek attention just because the earth had traveled around the sun one more time since she was born. But it wasn't another birthday wish. *I ordered Chinese food for lunch. I've been practicing using chopsticks. Wait until you see. You'll be so proud of me.*

I'm always proud of you. Chopstick master or chopstick failure. Nicole responded.

Thanks!! Lunch at noon. Meet me outside at our picnic table.

Nicole sent a thumbs up emoji back.

Annie obviously had been practicing. She handled the chopsticks like a pro.

"I'm very impressed," Nicole said. "You are a woman of many talents."

"I'm glad you finally noticed," Annie said.

"Oh, I noticed a long time ago. I just didn't want you to notice that I was noticing."

Annie even managed to get a pile of fried rice on her chopsticks and got it to her mouth without dropping a grain. "I didn't notice. So, mission accomplished."

Nicole laughed. She really did enjoy Annie's company. Maybe more than she should. Yeah. Definitely more than she should.

❖

"Surprise!"

Nicole walked into her house—Lisa's house, to a roomful of people. Surprise was an understatement. Lisa hadn't mentioned her birthday and Nicole had assumed that she had forgotten.

"Happy birthday, honey," Lisa said. She gave Nicole a kiss on the cheek.

She hadn't had a birthday party since she was seven. Besides her family, and Lisa's family, there were several friends, and Sandy and Jean recording every second. Of course. Nicole half-expected to see Annie there and was disappointed when she realized she wasn't.

"How's it feel to be the big three-two," Marley said as she gave her a hug.

"Not much different than it felt to be thirty-one."

"We're still on for dinner next week. I got Lisa's permission."

Nicole laughed. "Lisa said I could go out to dinner with you?"

Lisa winked at her. "I did. You're a big girl. I figured you could go out without me. This once," she added with a smile.

"Gee thanks. I appreciate it."

"It's the least I could do. And I always like to do the least I could do."

"I've said it before. I'll say it again. I like this one," Nicole's mom said. She put an arm around Lisa's shoulder. "You should keep her."

Keep her? Keep her as a friend? Definitely. Keep her as a wife? The jury was still out on that one. So far, the right feelings were evading her. She thought maybe Lisa was feeling the same way. At least she hoped she was.

"Hey, old lady." Ted came up and hugged her from behind.

"Who you calling old, big brother?"

"Oh, come on now. I'm just teasing ya. I know you're still young and hardly decrepit at all."

"Gee. Thanks for that."

"Cake and ice cream in the dining room," Lisa announced. "Then presents."

"I get presents?" Nicole asked in her best little girl voice.

"If you behave yourself, you do."

"Then I guess I'll behave myself."

"Good answer. Now let's go eat cake."

Someone pushed a glass of wine in her hand. Nothing goes better with carrot cake—her favorite—than a glass of white wine, Nicole mused.

After a rousing round of "Happy Birthday to You," Nicole cut the first slice of cake and handed it to her mother. Lisa took over the cutting and serving.

"How did you know I love carrot cake?" Nicole asked Lisa when she handed her a slice on a small plate.

"I have my ways. I want to know everything about you. Your likes, your dislikes, what makes you laugh. What makes you cry."

"Carrot cake makes me cry. In a good way."

"I don't see any tears," Lisa said.

"I'm crying on the inside."

"Is it really the carrot cake doing that or the fact that you hate attention, and you are being showered with it right now?"

"See, only married two months and you *do* know me."

"I also know you like vanilla ice cream," Lisa said, adding a dollop of it to the plate of cake Nicole was holding.

"Happy birthday, young lady." Lisa's dad came up behind her. "Were you surprised?"

"Thank you. Yes. Your daughter is full of surprises."

"She is. Like telling us she was marrying a stranger. That was quite the surprise. I'm glad the stranger was you. You two seem to make a great couple. I appreciate that."

Guilt creeped in around the edges. Not only had Lisa been hoping for love, but her family had hoped that for her too. And Nicole couldn't blame them. Lisa deserved that. Nicole was sorry she couldn't seem to give that to her. Lisa handed him a piece of cake and he went off in search of his wife.

"What's that look for?" Marley asked Nicole.

"What look?"

"I don't know. You looked—I guess sheepish is the word. What were you just thinking?"

"I was wondering what night we're going out to dinner." Nicole spooned some rapidly melting ice cream into her mouth.

"Yeah. That wasn't it. But I'll drop it. How does tomorrow sound?"

"Tomorrow sounds like it would work. Should I pick you up after work?"

"No. It would be easier to meet there. We can work out the details later."

Each person in turn wished Nicole a happy birthday and spent a few minutes chatting. There were a few gag gifts, including hand towels from her friend Jennifer that said LESBIAN LODGE in big bold letters. "We'll hang those in the bathroom," Lisa said. "So we never forget where we are." That brought a round of laughter.

Lisa's gift brought tears to Nicole's eyes. It was a ring. Gold with a modest diamond surrounded on each side by smaller diamond chips.

"We never had an actual engagement. But I wanted you to have an engagement ring," Lisa said.

Nicole was on her feet in an instant and pulled Lisa into a tight hug. "Thank you. It's beautiful." She wasn't sure if the tears were out of sentiment or guilt. Probably both.

All in all, it was one of the best birthdays that Nicole could remember. There might have been one or two better ones, but she'd gotten so wasted a couple of birthdays in her early twenties that she couldn't remember them.

"Thank you," she said again to Lisa once everyone had left. "I really appreciate what you did for me."

"You deserve it. Did you have a good time?"

"I did." She gave Lisa a kiss on the cheek.

"I have some chicken and a salad in the fridge for you. I don't think that cake was a sufficient dinner."

"Cake and ice cream is an ideal dinner. But I wouldn't mind something more if you'll join me."

They enjoyed a quiet meal together and then headed to bed. To sleep. Nicole was relieved Lisa didn't expect more.

❖

"And how have your first two months of marriage been?" Annie asked Lisa. Jean was getting the long shot from across the room and Sandy had her camera fixed on Lisa.

"So far so good," Lisa said. "Nicole is great."

"I understand you had a little bit of a monkey wrench thrown in your lives when you discovered a note written by another woman." It was a shitty thing to say, but it needed to be addressed. It was never fully resolved on any of the camera footage. At least this gave Lisa a chance to explain it.

"We did. I got mad at first, but Nicole later explained that it was an old note from months ago, a long time before we met. She has proven to be a very honest person. I have no reason not to believe her."

That was what Annie was hoping for. Closure. The audience wouldn't be left hanging with no answers to how the argument was resolved.

"That's good. No marriage is smooth sailing a hundred percent of the time. Are you finding any problems with Nicole? Anything that annoys you or things you would like to change?"

"As a matter of fact, yes."

Annie tried not to smirk. She wasn't sure she was successful. Now they were getting somewhere. It couldn't be all smiles and roses all the time. "Go on."

"Yesterday was Nicole's birthday and she ate all the extra frosting from the lid of the cake box. Everyone knows that's the best part." She laughed.

Yesterday was Nicole's birthday? Annie wished she had known. She would have had a little celebration at work. Gotten her a present and flowers.

They wrapped up the interview without Lisa giving up any juicy details, much to Annie's disappointment. And relief.

"Happy birthday, a day late," Annie said to Nicole once it was her turn to be interviewed. "I'm always a day late and a dollar short."

"I can lend you a buck if you need it," Nicole responded with a smile.

"I think I'll be okay till payday."

"Okay. Don't say I never gave you anything."

"I would never. You have given me a lot," Annie replied, turning serious. "Ready for some questions?"

"Shoot."

"You've been with Lisa for about two months now. Halfway there. How are you feeling about it?"

"Couldn't be better."

"Care to elaborate?" Jealousy. That was what Annie was feeling. She was jealous that things were going so well for them. Jealous that Lisa had Nicole.

"We get along great. Lisa has made a beautiful home here. And…" Bruce pushed open the bedroom door and bounced into the room. "And then there's Bruce here. He's just a bonus." She roughed up the fur on the big dog's head.

Lisa came rushing out of the bedroom. "I'm sorry," she said. "Come on, Bruce. It's Nicole's turn to say nice things about *me*. You're interrupting her interview." She took hold of his collar and steered him back to the bedroom.

Annie could hear Sandy snickering behind her. She turned to give her a stern, *be quiet*, look. Editing out extra noises from the final cut of the footage wasn't always easy.

There were no more interruptions and they finished in record time. There didn't seem to be any problems in the new marriage. Two months in, they were still in the honeymoon phase. Nicole's algorithms must be spot-on. So far it seemed like a match made in heaven. Both Nicole and Lisa had skirted around any questions aimed at finding out the level of intimacy they were sharing. Annie had no idea what was happening in the bedroom. Not that she wanted to know personally. The questions were to give the future audience a better insight into Nicole and Lisa and their marriage. They needed to feel invested in them and their happiness. The success of the show depended on it. At least that's what she told herself.

❖

"Are you and Lisa sleeping together?" Annie came right out and asked Nicole the next day at work.

"Good morning to you too." Nicole put her briefcase down on her desk. "I thought sleeping in the same bed was a requirement."

Annie swallowed and took a breath to gather herself. "I know it's none of my business, but for the sake of the show, are you two having sex?"

Nicole planted herself in her chair and leaned back. "Why would the sake of the show rest on whether we are having sex or not? I'm a little confused here."

Annie plopped down in the chair across from Nicole. She hadn't planned on asking her this way but found she couldn't help herself when she was face to face with her. Yes, she needed to know for the show, the audience needed to know. But she wanted to know as well. A part of her was holding out hope that maybe the marriage wouldn't work out. Maybe… No. She couldn't go there. "The viewers are going to want to know."

"It's none of their business. Wouldn't it actually be better to keep them guessing?"

Annie had to think about that a moment. Maybe. But *she* still wanted to know. Needed to know.

"Annie, why are you really asking me this?"

"For the show."

Nicole leaned forward. "I don't think that's the real reason."

Annie was at a loss for words. She couldn't tell Nicole the truth. Couldn't tell her about her developing feelings. Couldn't get in the way of her marriage. "Maybe you're right," she said after several long moments of silence. "Keeping the viewers guessing could work."

Nicole tilted her head and squinted at Annie. What was it she wasn't telling her? Why was it so important to her whether or not she and Lisa were doing the deed? She almost laughed out loud at her choice of words. She couldn't quite think of it as making love. Not with Lisa, because the love she had for her wasn't that kind of love. She wondered whether she should ask again for the real reason Annie wanted to know. But decided against it. She didn't want to admit to her that there had been no intimacy between them. She didn't want to let go of the charade of the happily married couple. She had a little less than two months to go before deciding whether to stay with Lisa or end it. A lot could change in that time. Not that Nicole thought it would.

"If you feel like talking about it, let me know," Annie said. "No pressure." She held up her hands and retreated to her own office without another word.

Nicole did her best to concentrate on her work, but Annie's question and the possible motivation behind it kept revolving around her brain. She hadn't gotten much done by the time she finally called it a day and drove to the restaurant to meet Marley for dinner.

"I still can't believe you're married," Marley said over drinks at the bar while they waited for their table.

"Me either."

"Why did you do it? I mean, you've never been the marrying type, let alone someone who would marry a stranger."

"Maybe I was just up for an adventure," Nicole said.

"Yeah. Still doesn't sound like you. What's the real story behind it?"

Nicole's thoughts teeter-tottered back and forth. She wasn't supposed to tell anyone the real reason. But Marley wasn't just anyone. She was Nicole's best friend. Family.

"Your table's ready," the hostess announced. "Please follow me."

Nicole grabbed her drink and trailed behind the hostess and Marley. The waitress arrived in record time and listed the specials for the night, leaving two large menus behind.

Marley set her menu on the table. "Nicole, what's going on? I get the feeling you're going through the motions with Lisa without anything real behind it."

Nicole couldn't help but smile. Her friend knew her very well. Maybe better than anyone else on the planet. "If I tell you, you have got to swear you won't tell anyone. Not even Ted."

"Of course," Marley said. "You know I can keep a secret. I never told a soul about that night in high school and the marching band."

"Oh my God, don't remind me."

"The point is your secrets are always safe with me."

Nicole started at the beginning, what her job entailed and how they were one bride short when it was almost time for the wedding.

"So, you just volunteered to get married? That is so not you."

"I didn't know what else to do. Without a bride we had no show, and without a show I didn't have my job. And, Marley, I love my job."

"And how about Lisa. Do you love her?"

The waitress was back at their table with order pad in hand. "All set?" she asked them.

"I'm sorry," Nicole said. "We need a few more minutes."

"Of course. Take your time." She disappeared into the backroom, or kitchen, or whatever was behind the swinging door.

"No," Nicole said and set about studying the menu.

"No what?"

Nicole tapped Marley's menu, still lying on the table.

They were ready with their orders for the waitress when she returned. "No what?" Marley repeated as soon as the waitress was out of earshot.

"No. I don't love her. At least not in the way you are supposed to love a spouse. I love her like a friend. I mean, she's a really good person. Anyone would be lucky to have her, but she's just not *my* person. You know what I mean?"

"Yeah. Have you told Annie that?"

Nicole shook her head and sipped her drink.

"Why not?"

"Because I've made it sound like everything is great. For the sake of the show."

"How about Lisa? Have you told her?"

"Not exactly. I mean, we've talked and decided it was still early. But I haven't really shared the fact that my feelings haven't grown."

The waitress arrived to fill up their water glasses.

"Thanks," Nicole said.

"Have you had sex?" Marley asked once the waitress left.

"That's exactly what Annie asked me today. Then she acted all weird about it."

"Weird about your answer?" Marley asked.

"No. I didn't actually answer it. I asked her why it mattered."

"Okay, back up here. What is the answer?"

"No. It just doesn't feel right. I mean, I'm all for casual sex, but sex with your wife is supposed to mean something."

Marley took a sip of her water. "And Lisa has been okay with this?"

"She hasn't made any moves either, so I'm thinking she is."

"So, the marriage isn't a real marriage."

Nicole hadn't thought about it that way. But Marley had a point. They seemed to be just going through the motions without any real feelings behind it. They certainly hadn't advanced much from where they started. She nodded. "That pretty much sums it up. But…" She let the word drift off, not sure if she should make any more confessions.

"But what? You can't start telling me something and then stop."

Nicole curled her lips in and shook her head.

"Nicole?"

"I think I have feelings for Annie," she blurted out, just as the waitress appeared with their fried mushrooms appetizer.

She placed a small plate in front of each of them. "Umm. Your meals will be out soon. Can I get you anything else?" she asked.

Marley glanced at Nicole and shook her head. "Thanks."

"Nice," Nicole said sarcastically. "Just what I need. More people knowing my secrets."

"Who the hell is she going to tell?" Marley asked. "Let's unpack this."

"You don't have feelings for Lisa, your wife. But you do have feelings for Annie, your boss."

"Pretty messed up, isn't it?"

"You said Annie got weird about the possibility of you and Lisa having sex. Do you think maybe she has feelings for you too?"

Nicole had never considered the possibility of that. No. She had never given any indication of that. But Nicole hadn't given her any indication either. What if she did? They couldn't act on it. Not only was she married, but so much of her life was being filmed. She was surprised and grateful that neither Jean nor Sandy had insisted on filming her having dinner with Marley. "I don't know. Maybe. But what does it matter?"

"I think you should talk to her. Ask her outright."

"No way." She stabbed a mushroom with her fork and dipped it into the horseradish sauce.

"Why?"

Nicole pulled her attention from the food on her fork and looked into Marley's eyes. "What is the point of that? If she says no, I just embarrassed myself. If she says yes, there is nothing we can do about it."

"Why not?"

"I'm married, Marley. That is supposed to mean something."

"We have already established that it's not a real marriage. How long is your commitment to this supposed to last?"

"Another two months. Then we make the decision of whether to stay together or get a divorce."

"Get a divorce," Marley said bluntly.

Nicole put the mushroom in her mouth and chewed slowly, keeping eye contact with Marley. She swallowed, feeling the heat from the horseradish travel to her sinuses. "It's not that simple."

"Why not?"

"What if Lisa doesn't want a divorce? What if she falls in love with me?"

"You're telling me you would stay married to someone that you don't love, when you have the possibility of being with someone you care about?"

It was a reasonable question. Except she wasn't sure there was a possibility of being with Annie. Ever. "I don't want to hurt Lisa."

"Let's pretend for a minute that you were madly in love with Lisa." Nicole started to object, but Marley put her hand up to stop her. "Just hear me out. If you loved Lisa and she didn't love you, would you want her to pretend to love you and stay married, so you didn't get hurt?"

"Maybe," Nicole said. "No."

"Then why would you do that to her?"

Marley had a point. Nicole had been play-acting for months and was starting to believe it. It was getting confusing. The one thing she wasn't confused about was that she couldn't tell Annie her real feelings. Not now. Maybe not ever.

Chapter Nine

"My turn to buy lunch today," Nicole announced in the doorway of Annie's office.

"You don't have to do that."

"If I *had* to do it, it wouldn't be any fun. And you know how much I love fun." Nicole smiled. It went straight to Annie's heart.

"Yes. I've heard you are a real party animal."

"Who has been spreading that ugly rumor?" Nicole asked.

"Me. It was me."

Nicole laughed. "Okay then. What and where would you like to eat today?"

Annie's mind went somewhere it shouldn't and she shook the thoughts away. She cleared her throat. "Umm…" She turned and glanced out the window. "Still raining so unless we want to get soaked and all wrinkly, the park is out. Conference room is in use today. I know I said we shouldn't be seen in public together, but I've been rethinking that." Okay, she'd just decided it was all right. Very little thinking involved. "How about we have lunch in the café on the first floor?" She had passed by the place on her way into work but had never eaten there.

"Are you sure that's a good idea?" Nicole asked.

"I am not. But there's nothing like the thrill of living dangerously once in a while. Right? But just to be on the safe side, let's have lunch a little later. That way we should miss the crowd."

"Okay," was her simple answer. "Two o'clockish?"

"Sure. Now get your ass to work." She couldn't help but watch that ass as Nicole turned and headed out the door to her office. So wrong. What the hell was wrong with her?

What are you doing? Annie asked herself. She had no answer. Her feelings were growing the more time she spent with Nicole. She was asking for trouble and trouble answered with a resounding *yes*.

As predicted, there was hardly anyone in the café at two. Annie was relieved. They ordered their food at the counter and made their way to one of the many empty tables.

"The network is going to start running commercials for the pilot along with the other shows premiering this fall," Annie said. She couldn't quite read the expression on Nicole's face. "What are you thinking?"

"To be honest, I'm not looking forward to my life being broadcast around the country."

Annie started to respond, but Nicole put her hand up, stopping her.

"I know. I'll get through it. It's just a season, right? It will be over soon, and I can go back to being the faceless person behind the computer." Nicole added two sugar packets to her tea and stirred.

"But it's such a beautiful face," Annie said. "It should be out there for all the world to see."

"Flattery will get you—a free lunch," Nicole said. "And..." She paused.

"And what?" Annie asked, truly curious.

Nicole let several beats go by before answering. "And a smile." Nicole's lips formed the sexiest grin.

"Then I will have to make a note to flatter you more often."

There was that smile again. That sexy, dangerous smile.

"If we're done talking about how beautiful I am—are we done with that?"

"For now."

"When are they going to show the pilot? Do you have a date yet?"

"Saturday, two weeks from tomorrow. I believe they are starting at eight and go until eleven with the new lineup. *I Do, I Don't* will be in the ten o'clock time slot. Can't have it on too early. Don't want to corrupt all those children with lesbian content." She attempted a sarcastic face but wasn't sure she pulled it off.

"I can understand that. Lesbians are one of the most dangerous groups on the planet."

"True. Followed closely by writers and murderers."

Nicole laughed. "I'm not sure I'm ready for fame."

"How about fortune? Are you ready for that?"

"I could deal with a little fortune. Might be able to buy myself some new underwear."

"Wow. You dream big. If you need new underwear, I could probably give you a raise," Annie said.

"I just figured I'll need some big girl panties once the show airs. I mean I'll have to deal with fans, autographs, stalkers. Stuff like that." She sipped her tea.

"You got this. I've seen how capable you are."

"With the computer maybe. But we are talking a whole new unexplored world."

"I've seen you with people. Your family. Lisa. Hell, even the way you treated the girl you ordered lunch from today. You're kind. You're funny. Everyone is going to love you."

"Even my stalkers?"

"Especially your stalkers." Annie took a bite of her BLT. She had been so wrapped up in their conversation that she had forgotten to eat. She noticed that Nicole hadn't taken a bite of her food either. "Is that something you are really worried about? Because I can get you a bodyguard."

Nicole shook her head. "No. I'm kidding about that. I'm sure it will be fine. I'm just not sure what to expect."

"I think your fame will be fleeting. I'm sure you would prefer it that way. Season one will air and then we're on to season two and a new set of celebrity brides."

"That would be good."

"You need to eat. Your french fries are getting cold."

Nicole squeezed a small puddle of ketchup onto her plate. "Maybe I like cold french fries."

"You do? That's just weird."

"No. I don't." She dipped a fry in the ketchup and took a bite. "Still warm."

"You know what they say. Warm fries, warm heart," Annie said.

"I think you got the quote wrong." Nicole held out her hand. "Cold hands, warm heart."

Annie looked at that hand—Nicole's hand—knowing it would be warm. Soft. She wanted to touch it. She pulled her attention from it and looked into Nicole's eyes. She was confused by what she saw there. Was it desire? The look disappeared as quickly as it appeared.

Nicole blinked, afraid if she looked too deeply into Annie's eyes she would get lost there. She put her hand in her lap. She thought for a moment that Annie might reach out and hold it. Nicole wasn't sure what she would have done if Annie had. She might be tempted to pull her across the table and kiss her for all she was worth.

"You're right," Annie said.

Nicole blinked again. Confused. She'd lost the thread of the conversation. "I am?"

"About the quote."

"Oh. Yeah. I usually am. Right."

"I figured that out a long time ago."

"Good to know. I have a feeling we will get along just fine."

Nicole wanted to get along better than *just fine*. She wondered if that was ever going to be possible after all this was over. After the marriage was over. She was pretty sure at this point that was where it was heading. But she wasn't ready to tell Lisa that and she sure as hell wasn't ready to tell Annie either. She wasn't ready to tell Annie about any of her true feelings. Yet.

❖

"I figured I'd find you working on a Sunday, sis," Terry said to Annie. She held up a paper bag. "I brought you supper. You've been so tied up in this show that I never see you anymore. And you look like you haven't been eating much either."

"Terry," Annie exclaimed. Her dark hair was longer than the last time she'd seen her. That must have been several months ago. She'd given her sister a tour of the offices when she first rented them, but this was the first time Terry had come by to visit. It was a pleasant surprise.

"Did you eat today?" Terry set the bag on Annie's desk.

"Does coffee count?"

"Nope. I've got your favorite." She pulled several things from the bag.

"Lobster thermidor? You're the best."

Terry laughed. "I am the best, but no. It's meatball subs and potato chips." She handed Annie her sub.

"My second favorite." She paused. "I mean lobster thermidor is my second favorite. This of course is at the top of my list and totally appreciated."

"Good answer."

"To what do I owe this pleasure?" Annie asked.

"Can't a girl visit her little sister, who has been locked up in her office for months and barely comes out to see the sunshine?"

"I saw the sunshine just yesterday." She unwrapped the food. The smell of the fresh sauce and cheese filled the air and made her happy.

"And what was yesterday?" Terry tossed a small bag of Lay's potato chips to Annie.

"I went and got a coffee refill at the coffee shop down the street. I glanced at the sun on my way there."

"More work. You know what they say about all work and no play?"

"It makes for good television?"

Terry tapped her chin. "I'm thinking that's not quite it."

"It's not forever," Annie said. "The pilot is in the can. The network is going to run it Saturday, filming for this season will be over in less than two months."

"Oh yeah. I saw a commercial for it. I thought the show was scheduled for October."

"They started running that promo yesterday. I haven't seen it yet. It is scheduled for October. They're showing several new pilots in September hoping to have an audience primed and waiting by the time the show premieres."

"And once this season is done and the show is a hit you'll already be working on next season. Right? When do you take a break?"

"Nic—I mean, my computer programmer is already working on the applicants for next season, so that part will be ready. I'll be able to take a break between seasons."

"Yeah, it will be the best twenty minutes of your life," Terry said sarcastically.

"Hey. I plan on taking at least thirty." She took a large bite of her sub and let the sauce wash over her tongue. It tasted as good as it smelled. "Besides," she said after she swallowed. "I like my work. It makes me happy."

"But it seems like it's all you do lately. How about fun? Dating? Having an actual life? I worry about you, sis."

"Don't. I'm fine."

"When was the last time you did something for yourself? Something you enjoyed. I mean besides work?"

Annie thought back to the lunch she'd had with Nicole a few days before. She certainly enjoyed that. Any personal time she spent with Nicole made her happy.

"What's that smile for?" Terry asked.

Shit. She didn't realize she was smiling. "Nothing."

"Spill."

What would it hurt to share a little? "I was thinking about the last thing—besides work—that I enjoyed."

"Which was?"

Annie took another bite of her food and took her time chewing it. "Beer?" she asked.

"Is that your answer? You enjoyed beer?"

"I'm asking you if you want a beer."

"Sure. And an answer to my question."

Annie rolled her chair over to the mini fridge against the wall and retrieved two bottles. She opened one, tossed the cap in the waste basket, and handed it to her sister.

"You think you're pretty cool dragging this out, don't you?"

"I do. Hey, that's the name of my show."

"I don't."

"Hey, that's the rest of the name of my show."

Terry shook her head and laughed. "Same crazy Annie. I love you. You know that?"

"I love you too." She opened her own beer and took a long swig. "And this beer. And this sub."

"Now that we've established that you're cool, tell me what you were thinking about when you smiled."

"I have been having lunch now and then with a very beautiful woman. I truly enjoy her company."

"Why you little sneak. How long has this been going on?"

Annie shook her head. "Nothing is going on. I just enjoy her company."

"Who is it? If you enjoy her so much, why do you say nothing is going on? I'm confused."

"She's married."

"Oh," Terry said. "Oh," she repeated. "That's not good."

"It's okay," Annie said. "We're just friends."

"Excuse me for saying this, but you don't smile that wide over a lunch with a friend. What gives?"

What gives was something Annie didn't want to admit, to herself or to her sister. "Nothing."

"You keep telling yourself that. But I can see it in your face. She means more to you than just a friend. Does she know how you feel?"

"No."

"What would happen if you told her?"

That was never going to happen. "I'm not getting in the middle of her marriage. It is either going to work or not work without me getting involved."

"Work or not work? I'm—wait. Is it one of the brides on your show?"

Was she that transparent? Would it help to deny it, or would Terry see right through that too?

"I can see the wheels turning in your head. I'm right, aren't I? Which one is it?"

"What do you mean, which one? You don't know who they are?"

"I saw the promo, remember. One had dark hair and one had dark blond hair. Which one did you fall for?"

"Oh my God. I didn't *fall* for anyone. I said I enjoyed having lunch with her." Maybe she had fallen for her, but she wasn't going to say that out loud. Time for a change of subject. "Are you going to eat or just leave that sub wrapped up?" Annie sipped her beer.

She watched as Terry unwrapped her food and took a small bite. Her strategy seemed to be working. "These are good. Where did you get them?"

"The blond or the brunette?"

Annie closed her eyes for several long seconds and found Terry staring at her when she opened them again. "The blond. Happy now?"

"The question is, are you happy?"

Annie had to think about it. "I'm happy when I'm with her. But it goes right back to the fact that she's married."

"How did this happen? I mean I know you've had to spend time with the women, but why are you having lunch with… What's her name?"

"Her name is Nicole, and she works for me." Why stop now when most of the cat was already out of the bag? To leave part of it out now would just be cruel.

"Works for you as in she is one of the brides?" Terry asked.

Annie shook her head. "No. She's my computer programmer. She developed the algorithm for matching the women."

"Wait. I want to understand this. Your programmer is also a bride? How did that happen? Is that ethical? And you *like* like her?"

Annie explained the situation and how Nicole came to be on the show and not just a faceless person behind the scenes.

"It wasn't anything we planned," Annie said. "But we had no choice. You can't tell anyone."

"Of course, I won't. But I have got to ask. If Nicole and the other bride—"

"Lisa."

"If Nicole and Lisa decide not to stay together at the end of the four months, will you tell Nicole how you feel?"

"I'm still her boss. It doesn't seem right." Annie took a couple more bites of her sub, scooping up a bit of sauce with her finger as it tried to escape the confines of the bun.

"Yeah, like no office romance ever happened between boss and employee. You're both adults, Annie. If Nicole returns your feelings, you should go for it. There isn't a reason not to. I know you, sis. You're not the kind that would take unfair advantage or pull some sort of power play."

"I'm not."

"How much longer till the four months are up? Until they decide if they are staying together or splitting up?"

"About a month and a half," Annie answered.

"Are you seeing any signs of trouble between them? I mean do they seem happy?"

Unfortunately, yes. They seemed happy. "They get along well," she said instead of sharing her real thoughts.

"A lot can happen in that time." Terry tilted her bottle of beer toward Annie and then took a swig."

"I'm not holding my breath. It would probably be better for the show if they stay together."

"But not for you."

"The success of the show *is* what's best for me."

Terry put her bottle down so hard on the desk that beer splashed out.

"Hey. Watch it." Annie moved a file from the edge of her desk to the filing cabinet behind her.

"When are you going to put life before work? I hate seeing you pouring yourself into this and making it your everything."

Terry's apparent anger took Annie by surprise.

"Why are you so pissed off?"

"Because I love you and it's hard to watch. Not that I've seen you lately. But I know you've put this show before everything, including your health and your love life. You know it's pretty ironic that you are trying to find love for other people but neglect it in your own life. What are you afraid of, Annie?"

"I'm not afraid of anything." She pushed the rest of her food forward. Her appetite suddenly gone.

Terry shook her head. "I don't understand you."

"I'll tell her. Okay?" *Wait. What?* Why did she say that?

"You'll tell Nicole about your feelings?"

"Yes. Are you satisfied?"

"When?"

"What?"

"When will you tell her?"

Annie felt like she was backed into a corner and instead of coming out swinging, she shrunk back and gave in. That was so unlike her. "I'll tell her if she and Lisa don't stay together."

"You need to tell her now. Give her the choice between Lisa and you."

"How fair is that? She needs to stay the course she started. The show won't work if she has someone else on her mind."

"So, you think she might share your feelings?"

"I didn't say that."

"Then why would she have someone else on her mind?"

"It would still be confusing for her. Hell, it's confusing for me. Can we just drop this? I said I would tell her if she and Lisa split up."

"I'm going to hold you to that," Terry said.

"What are you going to do? Pull my ponytail like you did when we were little, and I didn't do everything you demanded?" She smiled at the memory.

"Maybe. And I never demanded you do anything. I merely made strong suggestions."

"Like the time you *suggested* that I taste the mud pie we made?"

"I had forgotten about that. You never did tell me how it tasted."

"Sort of like mud, with a few pebbles mixed in."

"How come you never told on me?" Terry asked.

"Because I could never stand to see you punished."

"Ditto. That's why I hate this so much. I feel like you're punishing yourself. But I'm not sure why."

Maybe it was because she felt sorry—guilty—for using Nicole as one of the brides, even though it was Nicole's idea. And now she had to just stand by and see how it played out.

Chapter Ten

Nicole set her beach chair next to Lisa's, sat down, and dug her toes into the sand. Warm on the top, but cool underneath. That must be a metaphor for something, but at that moment, Nicole wasn't sure for what. She looked out at the lake, deep blue and mostly calm with an occasional random wave crashing on the shore. She tugged at the hem of her shorts, adjusting them. Wasting time. Delaying the conversation she knew was inevitable. Sandy had followed them to the beach but was off in search of a bathroom. So, it was now or never.

"Can we talk?" Nicole asked Lisa.

"Sure. We should be able to talk about anything. What's on your mind?"

Nicole watched the foam at the water's edge swell up, only to get dragged back into the lake and disappear again. She had rehearsed this conversation repeatedly in her mind over the last several days but wasn't sure how to start now that the moment of truth was upon her. The moment of truth. It was all about the truth wasn't it. Not that there had been total truth in their relationship.

"Nicole?" Lisa took her hand. "Everything okay?"

Nicole pulled her attention from the lake and her thoughts and looked at Lisa. "That depends on how you are going to take what I'm about to say."

"Oookaaay," Lisa said, stretching the word out.

"We have just about a month left to go before we have to decide whether to stay together or not."

"Yes."

"We've had three months together. I have enjoyed spending time with you."

"Me too."

"But, Lisa, I'm just not feeling the things I'm supposed to be feeling."

Lisa took several long beats to answer. "I don't think there are feelings you are *supposed* to have. You either have them or you don't. You can't force them."

"I don't think they're going to change in the next month. How are you feeling about this? About me?" Nicole was almost afraid to hear the answer. She didn't want Lisa to be hurt because of her.

"I like you a lot. Given more time I might fall in love with you. But right now, I'm not. And I won't let myself if you aren't in this completely."

"Lisa, I've tried to be in it completely. To get where I need to be to make this last."

"And that's all I could ever ask of you. You can't do more than that. I don't want you to pretend to feel things you don't."

"Where do we go from here? Do we keep pretending for the cameras?"

"Is that what you've been doing? Pretending?"

Nicole thought about it for a few seconds. Yes, there was some pretending. But pretending under the guise of fake it till you make it. "What I was doing was *trying*. Trying to make it work. Trying to get the feelings going."

Lisa squeezed Nicole's hand. "I appreciate that you tried."

Nicole shook her head. "What the hell is wrong with me? You are so perfect. Any woman would be lucky to have you."

Lisa laughed. "I am far from perfect. I've just been on my best behavior lately. And I'll settle for being friends with you. If that's what you want."

"I would like nothing more. I cherish you, Lisa. Please believe that."

"The feeling is mutual, Nicole. Don't feel bad for telling me the truth. I went into this hoping to finding my soul mate. But I also had my eyes wide open and knew that I might not. I'm not giving up on love. My someone is out there. Somewhere. I'll find her sooner or later." She paused. "Yours is too. If that's what you want. You signed up for this just like I did, so I assume you were hoping for love."

That was the thing. She didn't sign up for this hoping for love, not really. She just wanted to save the show and help Annie. But somewhere along the way she *started* hoping for it. But Lisa wasn't the person she was hoping to love. Not anymore. Annie's face floated through her mind. She pushed it to the back of her awareness. She wasn't planning on leaving her there forever. But she needed to get through this with Lisa first.

"Come on." Lisa pulled Nicole to her feet just as Sandy reappeared with her camera. "The water is calling our names."

"I didn't hear anything," Nicole said.

"It was sign language." Lisa ran a bit ahead. Her two-piece bathing suit showing off her perfect body.

"Yep," Nicole said under her breath. "I'm an idiot." An idiot who wanted someone else. Someone who had no idea. Someone who probably didn't return her feelings. Someone she would have a long talk with as soon as this marriage was over.

The water was cool against Nicole's skin, and she dove in as soon as it was thigh high. Lisa, a few feet ahead of her, stopped swimming, turned back to Nicole, and splashed water at her.

"Hey."

Lisa nodded in Sandy's direction, standing on the shore with her camera aimed at them. "We're under surveillance again. We should make it good."

"Are we fighting or getting along in this scene?" Nicole asked, sure that the sound of the water and wind would make their conversation impossible for the microphone to pick up.

"Let's do both. Playful at first and then you can get mad at me for being too rough."

"I like the way you think." Nicole realized that she could stand and touch the bottom. She pulled Lisa into her. Lisa wiggled away and splashed her again. "Oh no, you don't." Nicole dived toward her, and Lisa swam out of her reach. Nicole dived again and grabbed her around the waist.

Lisa planted a hard kiss on her mouth. She was confused for a moment then leaned into the kiss. Pretending. Lisa broke the kiss and somehow positioned herself behind Nicole, leaped onto her back, and pushed her underwater. Nicole came up spitting and sputtering.

"Get mad at me and go back to shore," Lisa whispered in her ear. "Yell at me when you get there."

Nicole shook her off and dove toward land. Lisa followed close behind, matching her stroke for stroke. Nicole switched to walking when she was closer to the shore. Sandy was right at the water's edge.

"What are you doing?" Lisa called to her.

Nicole turned around. She smiled, knowing Sandy could only film her from the back. "Why do you have to be so rough?" she yelled as loud as she could.

"Oh, come on. I was only playing."

Nicole steeled her expression and turned away from Lisa and continued back to their chairs. She plopped down in the sand.

Lisa caught up to her, stood with her hands on her hips, and stared down at Nicole. "I said I was just playing."

"I heard you. I don't like playing like that. Holding my head under water isn't fun for me."

"I didn't hold your head under. You must have slipped."

"Bullshit," Nicole said. *Guess Annie will have to bleep that out.*

Lisa sat in the beach chair. "I'm sorry that you thought I tried to hurt you."

"Oh. Sorry about what I thought. Not what you did?"

"Wow. You are just in a fighting mood today." Lisa kicked at the sand. "What's gotten into you?"

Nicole shook her head.

"Nicole, what's wrong? This isn't like you."

"Maybe you don't know me as well as you think you do." Nicole wasn't sure how long they should keep this up. Or how to start the pretend making up.

Lisa slipped off her seat and planted her butt in the sand next to Nicole. She took her hand. "I'm sorry. I would never do anything to purposely hurt you. I honestly was just messing around." She winked.

"You did hurt me."

"I realize that now. I'm sorry." Lisa was going to come out of this looking good. She made the apology seem sincere. She laid her head on Nicole's shoulder and looked up at her. "Please forgive me."

Nicole almost laughed but managed to stop it from bubbling out. "Are you going to make it worth my while?"

Lisa sat upright. "What did you have in mind?"

Nicole leaned over and whispered in her ear. "You are so good at this."

"Oh, you sexy little devil," Lisa said. "You got it. You know I would do anything for you."

"Anything?" Nicole said with a smile.

"Anything."

Nicole whispered in her ear again.

"You got it. Tonight will be a night you'll never forget." Oh yeah. Lisa was good at this.

❖

Annie stopped the footage when she saw Lisa kiss Nicole in the lake.

"What are you doing?" Lace asked. "We aren't to the good part yet."

"I need a break." Annie pushed her chair back. There hadn't been much on-camera affection between Nicole and Lisa, but this seemed different. It was hard for Annie to watch. Whatever the *good part* was, Annie needed to steel herself before viewing it. "Give me ten minutes." She was up in an instant and on her way outside.

This was all about the show, she reminded herself. Just the show. Personal feelings should never play into business. That was surely a recipe for disaster. She sat at the same picnic table she and Nicole had had lunch on several times. Those lunches had surely been a mistake. Getting to know Nicole better was a mistake. It had clouded Annie's feelings. Invaded her thoughts. She couldn't have that if she wanted this reality show to work. And she did want it to work. Wasn't that what her life was all about? The success of the show and Annie's career?

Terry would be pissed if she could read Annie's mind right now. And maybe she had a point. There was more to life than work. There was Nicole. But Nicole seemed to be in love with Lisa. So that put her right back where she started. Work was her life.

Her only life. She took a few more minutes to clear her head before she made her way back into the building and up to her office. "Come on. Break's over," she said to Lace. "Let's get back to business."

Lace hit *play* on the computer. Annie kept her eyes glued to the screen and her emotions tucked safely away. She was surprised when Lisa's playfulness led to an argument with Nicole.

But she didn't let it affect her one way or the other. She couldn't hear what they were saying until they were almost back to shore.

As quickly as the argument started, they made up, and from the looks of it, they had plans for that night to make up even more. As hard as she tried, she couldn't stop her stomach from flipping.

"You okay?" Lace asked her. "You look white as a ghost."

"I think ghosts are actually transparent. Or translucent. I get those two things mixed up."

"We got some great footage here," Lace went on. "Just about the whole scene is usable. I wish Jean had been there to get individual close ups, but we can do that ourselves in editing."

"Can you edit this segment?" Annie asked. She'd never let Lace edit by herself before, but she wasn't sure she could watch it again.

"Absolutely. I've got this."

"Good. I doubt it, but see if you can squeak the sound out of the footage when they're in the water."

"I'll do my best."

"I'm going to call it a day. Feel free to leave once that scene is finished. Upload it to the file for episode thirteen." Lucky thirteen.

"You're leaving while it's still daylight? That's a first."

"I need a drink and beer isn't going to cut it."

"Good for you. Have a nice time. I've got this."

Annie drove home and walked the two blocks to the little bar on the corner. She didn't want to have to worry about how much she drank or how to get home. Getting drunk wasn't something she had done since she was in her early twenties. Not that she planned on getting drunk now, but it wasn't entirely out of the realm of possibility.

The bar was dimly lit and nearly empty. It was too early for happy hour and the few people that were in there were scattered about. Annie took a seat at the far side of the bar.

"What can I get you?" the female bartender asked. Her hair was the same color and length as Nicole's. Great. She was here to forget about Nicole, not be reminded.

"Rum and Coke." She slid her credit card across the bar. "Start a tab. Please."

Three drinks later, the place was starting to fill in around her. The redhead that had taken the barstool next to her was cute. Late twenties, Annie guessed. At least she didn't look like you know who.

"Hello there," Annie said. "Do you like girls?" She was more than a little tipsy, well on her way to roaring drunk.

"I like everyone," the redhead answered. "But women more than girls."

"I'm a woman." Annie did her best not to slur her words. "Let me buy you a drink." She summoned the bartender over. "I'll have another one of these." She held up her glass. "And get whatever this beautiful lady would like."

"Gin and tonic. Top shelf."

"Oh," Annie said. "A woman with good taste."

"And that taste's good."

Annie wasn't sure she'd heard her right. Could she possibly be that blatant?

"Too much, too soon?" The woman laughed.

"Never," Annie answered.

"Good to hear." The bartender returned with the drinks. "Keep them coming," Ms. Redhead said to her.

The bartender placed her attention on Annie and raised her eyebrows with an unspoken question.

"Sure. Whatever the lady wants," Annie said. It seemed like it could be her lucky day. A few drinks was a small price to pay.

"Come here often?" the woman asked.

"Nope. You?"

"First time. I'm visiting from West Virginia. My friend is still at work, so I thought I would see what the night life is like around here."

"Not quite night yet." *Very witty. Way to impress the lady.* "Do you have a name?" What a stupid way to ask. Annie didn't know if it was the alcohol or if it was that she was so out of practice that it made her sound like an idiot.

"I'm pretty sure everyone has a name."

"Yes. I've heard that rumor too." She sipped her drink. More liquid courage might help. Picking up women in bars had never been her strong suit. "I have a name." Was she slurring her words or were her ears deceiving her?

"And what would that be?"

Annie briefly considered making up a name. She had been warned about strangers in bars. She was pretty sure that lecture from her mother when she was fourteen was more about men strangers. "Annie. My name is Annie."

"Nice to meet you, Annie." She held up her drink. "To women who know their own names." She took a long sip.

"I'll drink to that." Annie let the cool liquid warm her. How ironic she thought, staring into her glass. How did an ice-cold drink feel warm in your stomach? She was more than just a little drunk. She watched—what was her name? Did she say it and Annie had forgotten already? She was having trouble getting her brain to focus. "What do you do in Virginia?" Annie asked, hoping the woman's name would come to her.

"West Virginia. Whole different state."

"Yes. Yes, it is. You're right. Sorry."

"No problem."

"We get that, too. Ya know?"

"Get what?"

"New York. Someone asks where you're from and you say New York."

"I don't get it." She sipped her drink, eying Annie over the rim of her glass.

"They assume you are from New York City. Like that is all there is to New York. Like the rest of the state doesn't exist. But we do you know. Exist." Was she making any sense?

"Oh."

"Want to get out of here?" Annie could be as blatant as the redhead had been.

"Now why would we want to do that? The party's just gotten started." She finished her drink—that was fast—and ordered another.

Annie looked down at her near empty glass. Where had her drink gone? One more and she was sure she would go from drunk to shit-faced. Was shit-faced a good idea when she was trying to pick someone up? That begged the question, why was she trying to pick someone up? She had feelings for Nicole. Having sex with some random stranger—even someone as pretty as—what was her name—would only be a Band-Aid that would hurt like hell when it was pulled off. What did that even mean? She didn't know. She was here to forget about Nicole. *Nicole and Lisa sitting in a tree...* How did that child's song go?

"Another one?" the bartender asked.

Was she allowed to get another drink? Wasn't there some law that said they couldn't serve her more than X number of drinks? What did the X stand for? "Sure," she heard herself saying. She knew she was going to pay for this in the morning. It probably wasn't worth it seeing the goal was to forget about Nicole and it wasn't really working.

A tall man with a mustache sat down next to the redhead and gave her a kiss. What the hell. "Hey, baby," he said to her.

"How was work?" she answered.

Was this the friend she had mentioned earlier? Why was she kissing her friend on the mouth? What kind of friend was he? Annie's head was swimming. The choice to take this woman home with her had been taken out of her hands. It was probably for the best anyway. It wouldn't have taken away her longing.

"I'm going to get going," she said to the woman's back.

She turned. "Thanks for the drink." She held up her glass.

"Do you need me to call you a cab?" the bartender asked. Where had she just come from?

"Nope. No. Thanks. I live near here. I'm walking." She left her untouched drink and stood, waiting for the room to stop spinning.

"I need this signed." The bartender slid her credit card and receipt toward her. She had forgotten about that.

The night air was warm against Annie's hot skin. Drinking always raised her body temperature by a few degrees. Or did it lower it making her feel hotter? She wasn't sure and she was in no condition to care.

She walked with purpose toward her house, careful not to trip on any dips or ridges in the sidewalk. She fumbled with her keys, but managed to let herself in. Water. Water would help lessen the hangover she was bound to have tomorrow. She got herself a glass, stripped off her clothes and climbed into bed. Phone. Where was her phone? She slid out of bed and found it on the floor. It must have fallen out of her pants pocket.

She pulled up Nicole's name in her contact list and typed out a text. *I almost slept with a redhead tonight I don't know if I know her name. But do not worry. I didn't!! I think about you too much*

She hit send before she had a chance to change her mind and turned her phone off. She needed sleep as much as she needed Nicole to know that nothing had happened. That was important.

❖

"What's going on?" Lisa asked Nicole. "You have a strange look on your face. Who was that text from?"

"Annie."

"Setting up another interview?"

"No. I'm not sure what it's about."

Lisa didn't ask what the text said, and Nicole didn't volunteer it. She was thankful there were no cameras following their every move. Jean had left early. Guess she got tired of filming them hanging out on the couch watching TV. "I think I should call her. See what she wants."

"Of course."

Nicole hit Annie's name and listened as it went directly to voice mail. "Hey, Annie. Just checking on you. Everything okay? Give me a call as soon as you get this."

"No answer?" Lisa asked.

"No." She typed out a quick text to Lace. *Just got an odd text from Annie. Any idea what's going on with her?*

A response came a minute later. *She was acting kind of weird at work today. Left early. Said she needed a drink. Maybe she had more than one.*

Thanks. Nicole typed out. *Let me know if you hear from her, please. I'm a little worried.*

Lace sent a thumb's up emoji back.

That made sense. Sort of. If Annie was drunk-texting it would explain the message—to a point. What did *I think about you too much mean*? Annie thought about her? Too much? Was it more than just a boss thinking about an employee or one of her reality show players?

It was so hard, if not impossible, to decipher the tone or meaning from a text. And Annie's texts were usually perfect. This one had all kinds of errors. If she didn't hear back from Annie tonight, she would just have to ask her in the morning.

CHAPTER ELEVEN

Annie's head was pounding when she opened her eyes to the blinding sunlight that poured in through her bedroom window. Why hadn't she pulled the blinds before going to bed? Better yet, why did she drink so much? Details from the night before flickered through her brain like an old movie with parts too degraded to see.

Rum and Coke. Too many. A redhead. A guy. Walking home. Not much more. She looked around for her phone to check the time. She found it on the nightstand. The battery was almost dead. Apparently, she hadn't had enough sense to put it on the charger. There was a voice mail from Nicole. She hit speaker and listened.

What the hell? Why was Nicole checking on her? What had she done when she was under the influence of rum? Oh my God, she hadn't called her, did she? No. No outgoing calls from the night before. But there was a text. To Nicole. *Shit.* How was she going to explain that?

She flipped back to the home screen. Seven fifteen. Still time to shower, dress, and get to work. Not that she had to be there by a certain time. She was the boss after all. The boss with a splitting headache.

She downed a couple of Advil from the bathroom cabinet and stepped into a steaming shower. She let the hot water rush over her head and down her body. She'd screwed up, sending that text. What the hell had she been thinking? That was just it. She hadn't been thinking. She'd let her heart overrule her head when she saw Nicole and Lisa kissing at the lake.

She needed to pull herself together and get her head out of her ass. This was just plain stupid. She was letting her feelings get in the way of her job. That had to stop. Now.

She gave her hair a quick wash and rinse, toweled off, and got dressed. Lace was already in her office reviewing the latest footage on the desktop computer in the corner.

"Morning, boss. You look like shi…" she paused. "Rough night?"

"You could say that." She found a bottle of Advil in her desk drawer and popped two more in her mouth. She swallowed them without the aid of water.

"Nicole sent me a text last night. She was worried about you. Said something about an odd text."

"I did." Nicole was leaning against the opened doorframe of Annie's office. "And I was. Everything okay?"

Annie was at a momentary loss for words. Not something she was used to dealing with. She looked from Nicole to Lace. "Lace, would you mind taking a break? I want to talk to Nicole for a few minutes." She hadn't figured out an acceptable explanation to give Nicole yet.

"Oh sure. No prob. I'll just be in my office if you need me. But it looks like you don't need me. So…"

Nicole turned sideways to let her pass and sat down in the seat she'd just vacated. "What's going on, Annie?"

Annie got up, shut the door, and leaned against it. She waited until she heard the usual music coming from Lace's office before speaking. "I was having a rough day yesterday, and well, I may have had too much to drink. And by *may*, I mean I did. Got myself drunk in fact."

"What did that message mean? You think about me too much? And what's with the redhead?"

"All good questions. I may have been flirting with a young woman who sat down next to me. I thought about taking it further but didn't." She hoped that was enough of an explanation.

"And the other part? Thinking about me too much?"

Annie wished Nicole would stop reciting the text. "I… umm…I guess I just worry that I pushed you into something that you didn't want to do." No need to explain more. She hoped.

"Annie, it was my idea. I'm a big girl. But I like Lisa and I'm glad she's in my life."

Like. Annie took the word and tossed it around in her head. Nicole said like, not love. Did that mean something? No. The kiss they shared in the water and the innuendo later meant something. She was grasping at imaginary straws.

"Is that really what you meant?" Nicole suspected there was more to this than Annie was letting on. She seemed distracted, like she was trying to skirt around the truth, but not out-and-out lie. The way she shifted her weight from one foot to the other and back again reminded Nicole of the tigers in the zoo that circled their enclosures time and time again with the understanding that they were trapped and there was no way out.

"That's my story and I'm sticking to it," Annie said with a nervous laugh.

It may have been her story, Nicole thought, but it wasn't her *whole* story. Of course, Nicole wasn't sharing her own story— her own feelings—with Annie either. If she did, would Annie's story change? Was Annie feeling what Nicole was feeling? Now was not the time to find out. She was still married, at least for another twenty-eight days. It might have been for the cameras, but Lisa was still her wife, at least legally. Morally too if you wanted to get technical. It wouldn't be fair to Lisa to profess her feelings for Annie. Not yet at least. "Okay," Nicole said.

"Okay?"

"Yeah." Nicole got up. "I better get back to work. That data isn't going to enter itself. Which is a good thing because I would be out of a job if it did." She walked the few steps to the door, but Annie made no attempt to move out of the way. "Annie?"

Annie's gaze went to Nicole's lips and for a moment, Nicole thought she was going to kiss her. And Nicole knew if she did, she wouldn't have stopped her. Not in that moment. Not with her so close she could feel the heat coming off her body. Annie's eyes traveled up to Nicole's eyes and locked there. Nicole could see the want in them. The need. She looked away, afraid of what she might do if she didn't. This couldn't happen. Not now.

"I'm sorry," Annie said and stepped aside.

Nicole opened the door and went to her own office. She shut her door, closed her eyes, and leaned her head against it. What the hell had just happened? What had almost happened? They almost kissed. They both wanted it. Nicole was sure of that. What she didn't know was what to do with it.

She realized that her underwear was wet. Actually wet from the *almost* encounter. What the hell? She kissed Lisa full on and felt nothing but had this kind of reaction from just the thought of kissing Annie?

She needed to get a handle on this. She sat at her desk and turned on her computer. She pulled the stack of applications from her top drawer and plopped them on the desk. She typed in the number on the top of the paper and a couple of personality traits. She found herself staring blankly at the screen. Her mind going again and again to Annie. There was no mistaking that look in her eyes.

She got very little work done and decided to leave work early. How stupid to get so hung up on what could have—almost happened.

"Let's go out to dinner," Nicole said to Lisa when she got home.

"What's the special occasion?"

"Do we need a special occasion to spare you from cooking? Besides, now that you're back to teaching you deserve a break."

"I'll take it. Let me go change and I'm all yours," Lisa said.

All mine? Definitely not. "If we hurry, we can leave before whatever camera woman was assigned to spy on us tonight."

"Ooh, that would be nice."

Nicole changed in the bedroom, while Lisa changed in the bathroom. They had been married a little over three months and had never changed clothes in the same room. Nicole knew some women who had no problem getting naked in front of friends or even strangers. She was never one of those people. It seemed that Lisa wasn't either.

"Table for two," Nicole told the hostess. It was too early for the dinner rush, and they were seated without waiting.

"How's this?" the hostess asked, handing them each a menu.

"Perfect." It was a place Nicole had been to before with friends and was always pleased with the food. "Thank you."

"Your waiter will be with you shortly to explain the specials and take your drink orders. Enjoy."

"This is my first time here," Lisa said.

"Great food."

"Excuse me," a stranger said coming up to the table. "I saw you on that new show. *I Do, I Don't.* You two are the cutest couple. Can I have your autographs?"

Nicole had forgotten the pilot episode had run on TV already. Both she and Lisa had agreed not to watch it. Annie told her it was better that way. She knew there would be some attention, but never thought it would start so soon. She wanted to shrink into the woodwork.

"Thank you, so much," Lisa said, taking the lead. "Of course. Do you have anything to write on?"

The woman patted her pockets as if she was searching for something. She grabbed a napkin from their table and stopped a waitress going past for a pen. "They are celebrities," she told her.

"Oh yeah. What movie?"

"TV show. *I Do, I Don't*. Aren't they just the cutest?" She shoved the paper in front of Nicole and handed her the pen.

Nicole looked at Lisa helplessly. Lisa smiled and shrugged.

Best Wishes! Nicole Hart She wrote and slid the napkin to Lisa. Whatever Lisa wrote was much longer than Nicole's effort.

"There you go. I hope you enjoy the show when the full season comes out next month. Tell all your friends."

The woman hugged the napkin to her chest. "I will. Thanks so much. I'll cherish this."

That lady really needs to get a life, Nicole thought. If this was the kind of attention she could expect she wasn't looking forward to it. Lisa didn't seem to mind. Then again, Lisa had signed up for this willingly and undoubtedly knew what to expect.

The woman turned and left with the waitress on her heels, probably trying to retrieve her pen.

"Didn't like that, did you?" Lisa asked.

"I guess I'm not the public figure type."

"You'll get used to it. Besides, it's only fifteen minutes of fame. It will pass and you can get back to your nice quiet life. I'm assuming when this is all over, you'll be going back to your apartment."

Nicole almost felt guilty saying yes. Almost. What she felt more was relieved. And *that* made her feel guilty.

"It's okay, you know. I knew I was taking my chances when I signed up for this. But I have got to tell you that I'm going to miss you. So is Bruce. I hope you stay in our lives."

Nicole reached across the table and took Lisa's hand. "Of course, I will. You've become important to me. And I've even gotten used to Bruce sleeping on my feet. I'll have to put some bricks at the foot of my bed to re-create the sensation." She smiled.

"I tried to get him to sleep on the doggy bed on the floor."

"I know you did, and I appreciate it. But that's been his spot for as long as you've had him. I don't blame him for wanting to sleep there."

A flash from a phone camera went off in Nicole's face and she blinked against the blinding white. "Hey. What the hell, dude?"

"A picture of the happy couple for the local newspaper. Not every day we get TV stars living in this town."

"Not true," Lisa said. "Richard Gere is from here and Tom Cruise was born here. True, he didn't live here long. But still. Oh, and Rod Serling."

"Who?" Nicole asked.

"You know. The guy from the original *Twilight Zone*."

Nicole wondered how she knew that. That show must have been on at least thirty years before she was born.

"Can I get a statement for the paper?" The guy held up his phone, ready to record.

Again, it was Lisa who took the lead. "It would be great if everyone tuned in to watch our journey on *I Do, I Don't* starting October tenth at ten p.m. Umm, that's Eastern Standard Time of course."

Nicole blinked at her. She seemed well rehearsed and obviously not a bit thrown by this like Nicole was.

The man moved the phone to Nicole. "And you, young lady."

"What she said."

"Aww, come on. You must have something to say for our readers."

"Go ahead, honey. You've got this," Lisa said.

Nicole tilted her head up as if there was something written on the ceiling that would help her out. There wasn't. "I have enjoyed this journey with Lisa. If you get the opportunity, I highly recommend you submit an application to be on this show. You never know what could come of it." There, that was the truth and would hopefully bring in even more women to choose from for future seasons. Annie would be pleased. Annie. Stop thinking about Annie.

"Great job," Lisa said. Lisa her wife. At least for another month. "What newspaper will this be in?" she asked the man.

"*Herald Journal* in print and online. It could get picked up by any number of newspapers across the country."

"Thank you. Now if you wouldn't mind leaving us, so I can enjoy a lovely dinner with my beautiful wife, I would appreciate it," she said much more politely than Nicole would have.

He nodded his head. "Certainly. Ladies." He made his way across the restaurant and sat at a table with several other people.

"Do you think we're being stalked?" Nicole asked.

Lisa laughed. "No. They are obviously just other diners who happened to see the show. I promise it won't be like this forever."

"How can you be so sure?"

"Because our season will be over, and they will move on to the next ones in line. We'll be old news."

"That can't come soon enough for me."

"You mean ending this marriage?" Lisa asked. Was that sadness in her eyes?

"I'm so sorry, Lisa."

"You don't need to be sorry. We tried. We don't click that way. And you've been honest with me. There is nothing more I could ask for."

"What the hell is wrong with me?" Nicole asked. "You are so great."

"You are too. We stay friends. You bring me out to dinner to nice places like this every once in a while." She waved her hand. "And we'll get along just fine."

"Deal."

The waiter, complete with a neatly pressed white shirt, black pants, and notepad arrived to take their drink orders and recite the well-rehearsed dinner specials.

Dinner, like the next three and a half weeks of their marriage, went smoothly. Nicole avoided being alone with Annie at work. No more lunches in the conference room or the park. They kept it very surface and professional when they did see each other. The show debuted to mediocre ratings.

It was time for the final interview, the one where Nicole and Lisa revealed their commitment to stay together or move on alone.

Annie had hired a third camera person to make sure they were filmed from every angle, and that Lisa and Nicole each had their own close ups. She was well aware of Nicole's reluctance to be alone with her since she'd made a fool of herself by almost kissing her.

Well, there was nothing she could do about that now. She had prepared herself for the interview she was about to do and the words that would more than likely cement Lisa and Nicole's relationship. At least she thought she had. Her stomach was still in knots, despite her best efforts at calming it, and her nerves, down.

All three of the camerawomen were in place and rolling and Lace had taken a seat across the room, out of camera range. Annie sat on a chair they'd pulled in from the kitchen, across from Lisa and Nicole who sat close together on the couch, holding hands. She put on her professional face and smiled. "Ready?"

They nodded in unison.

"Good. I need you to take your time answering the questions. Don't jump right in. The point is to build suspense for the audience. We need to draw this out."

"Got it," Lisa said.

She asked them some general questions about living together, the dog, Nicole giving up her apartment, and such. Each answer was upbeat and positive. Just what Annie suspected would be the case based on the footage she'd edited so far.

"Let this next question roll around in your head. Don't give away too much by your facial expressions. We are going to start with Lisa." She knew she would edit out her instructions and focus only on the question and each of their answers. Lisa's answer would be much easier to hear than Nicole's. Because who wouldn't want to stay married to Nicole?

"Lisa, now comes the big question. You and Nicole seem to have gotten along really well. Do you want to stay married or get a divorce?"

Lisa, as instructed, took her time to answer. She looked into Nicole's eyes and a tear ran down her cheek. Nicole wiped it away with her thumb while looking appropriately nervous. She played her part well.

Lisa cleared her throat. "Nicole," she said. "I love you."

The long pause that followed brought a fresh round of acid to Annie's stomach. She rolled her hand, indicating it was okay to go on.

"But…" Another long pause. "I want a divorce."

Wait. What? Annie didn't see that coming. As much as she wanted Nicole herself, she worried about the hurt this would cause her.

"When I say I love you, it's as a friend. I want to keep you in my life forever. But not as my wife. Can you understand that?"

It took forever for Nicole to respond, and Annie wished she hadn't asked them to drag their responses out.

Finally, Nicole nodded. "I do. Because I feel the same. I have enjoyed spending time with you and getting to know you. You feel like the sister I've never had and always wanted. This marriage has been great in so many ways, but it doesn't feel like we should be together as a couple."

Annie had lost the thread of the questions. She wasn't sure what to ask next. She hadn't expected this. They both turned to her. Waiting.

"I…" She stumbled. "Umm…"

Lace came up behind her. "Are you sure about this?" she said more to Annie than to Nicole and Lisa.

"Yes. Right." Annie cleared her throat. "Are you sure about this?" she asked them.

"I am," Nicole answered, as she focused her attention once again on Lisa.

"Me too," Lisa replied. "We gave it our best shot. I've learned so much these past four months. Not only about Nicole, but about myself too. What I want and need from a partner. I'm not willing to settle just because someone like Nicole is nearly perfect. She'll make the perfect wife for someone, some day. Just not the perfect one for me."

"I feel the same," Nicole said. "Whoever you end up with will be very lucky."

"What brought you to this conclusion?" Annie asked, not sure if they had already answered it. Her head was swimming, and it was hard to think straight. She didn't want to think about what it could mean for her and Nicole being together. Getting her hopes up could end in disaster and a broken heart.

"I just don't have the right feelings one should have for their wife," Nicole said.

"Ditto," was Lisa's response.

"Where do you go from here?" Annie asked, starting to get back in the rhythm.

"Back to my apartment. To my own life. Keeping Lisa in it as a friend."

"A friend I love and will always cherish," Lisa added. "Just because it didn't work out for us, doesn't mean it was a waste. I will always be grateful for our time together."

Annie asked a few more superficial questions and then wrapped it up. "I'll have my lawyer draw up the divorce papers so we can get this taken care of for you. I'm sorry it didn't work out," she said once the cameras stopped rolling. She wasn't really sorry it didn't work out. She wasn't sure what she felt. Relieved. Maybe. A little sad for them.

"Upload the final footage by tomorrow," she told Jean and Sandy. "Sandy can take care of yours," she said to the third camera person, whose name she had forgotten. How unprofessional was that? There was a lot about this that had become unprofessional. That was so unlike her. Her work had been her life for years. She was letting it slip because of her feelings.

"I suppose you'll be moving back to your apartment soon," she said to Nicole.

"Yeah. Probably tomorrow." She turned to Lisa. "I'll miss you. But I'll write every day."

Lisa gave her a kiss on the cheek. "A visit now and then would be good."

"You got it."

Annie packed up the little she had brought with her in her briefcase. "I wish the best for both of you. If you want to watch the show, it shouldn't be a problem now."

"I think I'll pass," Nicole said. "I lived it. I don't need to watch it, too."

"See you at…" She almost said *the office*, to Nicole. She caught herself in time. It still wouldn't be a good idea for Lisa to know that Nicole worked for her. "Umm, see you soon to tie up any loose ends."

She said her good-byes and was out the door, followed closely by the rest of the crew.

"You okay?" Nicole asked Lisa once they were alone.

"Yes. But I wasn't lying when I said I'm going to miss you. It has been great having you here. But you are probably anxious to get back to your real life."

"I'm going to miss you too, and my real life wasn't that interesting. I'm sure you'll keep yourself busy now that school is back in session."

"I will, but teaching isn't my whole life. I'm going to give myself a break for a little while and then put myself out there. I still want my person. My one and only, and I'm not giving up until I find her."

"I'm glad. You deserve the best, Lisa. I mean that."

"And how about you? Will you still be looking?"

Nicole hadn't been looking in the first place, but she might have stumbled onto it anyway. There was no way she could tell Lisa about her feelings for Annie. At least not right now. At some point she would tell her everything. Lying by omission to a friend wasn't something Nicole wanted to do. It had been hard enough not telling the truth to Lisa as her wife. "I don't know what the future holds for me. There might be someone. Somewhere. Some day. Only time will tell."

"How about we order a pizza and watch a movie our last night together? Celebrate the end of a marriage and the beginning of a wonderful friendship?" Lisa said.

"I would like that. I'll open a bottle of wine."

"Perfect," Lisa said. And it was.

Nicole had no idea what would happen on Monday morning when she went back to work, more or less a free woman. But she was curious to find out.

CHAPTER TWELVE

Annie was already in the office when Nicole arrived. She'd left her door open a crack purposely so she could hear Nicole's arrival. She gave Nicole a few minutes to settle in and then knocked on her door.

"Come on in."

Annie opened the door and leaned against the doorjamb. "How are you doing?" she asked. "Really."

Nicole looked up from her computer. "I'm fine. Really. I'm all settled in at my apartment again. It seems a little too quiet, but it's home."

"And Lisa?"

"Lisa seems good too. She has Bruce to keep her company. She hasn't given up on love and that's a good thing. I hope she finds someone wonderful."

"I'm sorry I put you through this," Annie said. *And myself as well.*

"You didn't. I'm glad I went through it. Lisa isn't the only one that learned about herself. I did too."

"And what did you learn?"

"That love can exist for people other than just my parents and fairy-tale characters. That there is more to life than work. Spending time with Lisa taught me how important relationships can be."

"Even though it didn't work out with her?"

"Oh, but that's the thing. It did work out with her."

Annie's heart sank.

"It just didn't work out the way it was originally intended. I have a friend for life."

Annie tried not to breathe a sigh of relief, but it slipped out anyway. "I'm glad," she said. She didn't have too many friends in her life. Her work had dominated everything. Maybe it was time to change that. Being so driven had brought her nothing but a few extra dollars and a lot of anxiety.

"Is it okay if I leave a little early today?" Nicole asked. "I want to swing by my parents' and let them know what's going on. My mom's going to be disappointed. She really liked Lisa."

"I'm sorry."

"You can stop saying that now. My mom and Lisa can still be friends. It's not the end of the world."

Annie laughed. "Okay. And of course, you can leave early. I need to finish the editing on the last two episodes, so lots to do. If I don't see you before you leave, I'll see you tomorrow."

Nicole nodded and Annie closed the door behind her.

She wasn't sure what to think anymore. Nicole and Lisa were no longer together as a couple, but after the way Nicole avoided her after almost kissing her, she didn't think Nicole was interested in her either. She said she believed love can exist. Something she didn't believe before. Did that mean she would be seeking it out? Loving people as friends? Or something else completely? Annie had no idea. She was more confused than ever.

Back in her own office, she reviewed some of the footage that Lace had marked and moved it to the appropriate folder on the desktop. The first fourteen episodes were edited. The pilot and second episode aired to less than stellar ratings, but that sometimes happened with new shows. It took the audience a while to find it and get hooked. Annie wasn't panicked. Yet.

At eleven thirty she ordered lunch via Grubhub and took a break to eat when it was delivered a half hour later. Other than the days she shared lunch with Nicole, she usually skipped meals. But Terry was right. All work and nothing else wasn't good for her. Step one, take care of herself with healthy meals. Step two, have an actual social life. That one was easier said than done. Step one would have to be enough for now. She could start working on the rest tomorrow. Or next week.

❖

Nicole knocked on her parents' door and then let herself in. It was seldom locked during the day when someone was home.

"Hi, honey," her mother said. "Where's Lisa? We were hoping you were going to bring her when you said you were coming over."

"That's kind of what I wanted to talk to you about. Where's Daddy?"

"Upstairs. He'll be down in a minute. Pull up a chair. I'll get you a glass of lemonade."

Nicole sat at the kitchen table. It seemed to be the room they gathered in the most. "Thanks."

"Hey, baby girl." Her father bounded into the room. Nicole hoped she had half his energy when she got to be his age.

Her mother poured two more glasses of lemonade, added ice, and set them on the table along with a plate of oatmeal cookies. "We're all here now. What's going on?" She sat in the chair at the end of the table and her dad sat in the chair opposite her.

"First of all," Nicole started. She had rehearsed her speech most of the day. "I know you love Lisa. I do too. Just not in the right way."

"What does that mean?" her dad asked. "Is there a wrong way?"

Nicole laughed. It helped cut the tension that had been building in her all day. "No. What I mean is, I don't love her the way you should love your wife. I love her like a friend."

"Well, doesn't that take time?" her mother asked. "I mean you've only known her for what, four months? That's not very long."

"How long did it take you to fall in love with Dad?"

"I was pretty head over heels by our third date."

"That's my point. These four months were very intense. I mean we have pretty much been together all the time, except when I was working. If I was going to feel something, I would have felt it by now." She wondered if she should mention that she had feelings for someone else. The *right* kind of feelings. She decided against it. For now.

"How does Lisa feel?" her dad asked.

"The same way I do. Like we are good friends. Nothing more."

"Oh, honey." Her mother rubbed Nicole's arm. "I'm so sorry it didn't work out. What happens now?"

"I'm okay with this. I really am. Now, we get a divorce. I know that's not what you wanted for me and I'm sorry. I know you're disappointed."

"We only wanted you to be happy. That's all."

"Lisa will still be in my life. You'll still get to see her." Nicole sipped her lemonade. As usual, it needed more sugar. She could never understand how they could drink it like that. As if reading her mind—or maybe her face—her father pushed the sugar bowl in her direction. She added a spoonful and stirred. "I already moved back into my apartment. I have to say it's good to be home." And sleeping in her own bed.

"Do Ted and Marley know?" her mother asked.

"Not yet. I'm going to run over there before I go home." She was hoping to catch Marley alone before Ted got home from work. "We need to keep this just between us until the final episode of the show airs. Have you watched any of it?" They hadn't mentioned it one way or the other.

"We watched the first episode. I think I looked good at the wedding, but I didn't like how I looked when you came over to tell me you were getting married. My double chin was all over the place," her mother said. "Your father looked good in his tux."

"Oh, my dear, you looked beautiful in all of it," he said to her.

"We started to watch the next episode, but it felt like we were watching your personal life, so I made your father change the channel. The Hallmark movie seemed much less intrusive."

Nicole chuckled to herself. Guess she shouldn't be making fun of those sappy movies anymore now that she had a starring role in a reality series. Who would have thunk it? Not her. That's for damn sure. But she did it and she survived. Yeah, she was getting attention from strangers on the street and even had a phone call from Entertainment Tonight for an interview, but it all seemed pretty harmless. She referred the reporter to Annie to deal with. She hoped Lisa was right and everyone would forget about her as soon as her fifteen minutes of fame was over.

She finished her lemonade, much better with the added sugar, hugged her parents good-bye, and headed over to Ted and Marley's house. Marley opened the door, still dressed in her work clothes.

"Can I get you anything to drink or snack on?" Marley asked.

"No. I'm all lemonaded out. I just came from Mom and Dad's." Nicole plopped herself down on the couch. "As you probably figured, Lisa and I are calling it quits. Annie is arranging for a divorce."

Marley sat next to her. "Can't you get it annulled? I mean you never had sex, right? Doesn't that qualify?"

"Nope. I looked it up. New York doesn't consider that a reason unless one of us is physically unable to and we didn't find out until after we were married."

"Well, that would suck. Finding out after you were married that one of you is frigid. I mean, not the point. Go on."

"Anyway, we wouldn't qualify for it. A divorce is actually easier."

"What are you going to do now?"

"Live my life the way I did before I got married."

"With one exception," Marley said.

"And what would that be?"

"Annie. What are you going to do about Annie?"

"I haven't figured that out yet. Any suggestions?"

"Yeah. Walk into her office and kiss the living shit out of her."

"Any other suggestions?"

"Walk into her office, throw her across the desk, and fu—"

"Not helpful." Nicole told Marley about the near kiss. "I think she has feelings for me too. At least in that moment she did."

"And now. What kind of a vibe are you getting?" Marley kicked off her shoes and pulled her feet up under her.

"I don't know. I've been mostly avoiding her since then. She knows Lisa and I are done. I couldn't get a good read on how she felt about that. So, my plan is to play it cool for a while. Try to figure out what to do. I haven't really been interested in a relationship, not for a long time anyway. But with Annie I feel different. Hopeful somehow."

"That's good. You've been alone too long."

Ted came strolling in the door and dropped his briefcase on the coffee table. "Hey, sis. Marley said you'd be stopping over. Haven't seen you much since you said *I do*."

"Well, now it's *I don't*."

He sat down across from them in the La-Z-Boy chair Marley had given him for Christmas two years ago. No one else was allowed to sit in it. At least while he was home. Nicole was pretty sure Marley sat in it when she got home from work before him. "Say what?"

"Name of the show. *I Do, I Don't*. I said I do. Now I don't. Lisa and I are separated. Heading for a divorce."

His face fell. "No. I thought you two were doing so good. What happened?"

Nicole was getting tired of telling the story, but she repeated it again for her brother. "We're still friends and we're both okay with this," she added.

"What can I do to help? What do you need? Help moving? Money for a lawyer? A drink? I could use a drink. And I don't have extra money for a lawyer."

Nicole laughed. Ted always had a way of making her feel better. Not that she felt bad. Relieved was a better word for it. "Thanks anyway. I'm going to get going. I want to turn on *my* TV and binge some mindless show for a while." Not that she really minded watching Lisa's TV with her.

"Call us if you need anything," Ted said. "Except for money. We've already gone over that."

"Thanks. I should be all set." She hugged them both good-bye and headed home. Her apartment seemed strangely quiet, even with the television on. She poured herself a glass of wine and plopped down on the couch, using the coffee table to stretch her legs out. Any thoughts of Lisa were replaced by thoughts of Annie. Nicole wondered what she was doing. It was still early. She was probably at work going through footage of her and Lisa's life in the last month. How strange that must be for her. How strange it was for Nicole to live it. What kind of thoughts and, more importantly, feelings did it stir in Annie?

❖

Annie noticed a slight shift in the interaction between Nicole and Lisa in the last month of their marriage as she ran through the video on her computer. The small gestures of affection seemed to all but disappear. Why hadn't she noticed that before? She made sure to include any that had happened between them in the final footage. She didn't want the audience clued in on the fact that they weren't staying together. Annie rolled that around in her head for the umpteenth time. Nicole was free, at least in spirit. Legally, it would take a little longer.

She knew she had to tell Nicole about her feelings, but now, so soon after she and Lisa ended didn't seem right. The divorce shouldn't take that long. Annie already had a lawyer drawing up the papers. There was nothing to divide and no spousal support, so it would be fairly simple.

She wrapped up the episode she was working on and decided to call it a day. Lace and Nicole were already gone for the day. She skipped the elevator and took the stairs down to the lobby. Outside, she blinked against the bright sunlight. When was the last time she left work this early? She didn't know.

"Hey, Terry," she said when her sister answered the phone. "Whatcha doing? Want to grab a bite to eat or a drink? Or better yet, both."

"Who is this?" Terry asked.

"Ha ha. Very funny."

"You never leave work this early."

"Yeah, well, you know someone said I should get a life. I guess I'm trying to."

"And you're starting with me. I'm honored. And I would love to get together. I just need to tie up some loose ends at work. Shouldn't take long. Your place or mine? Or better yet, what bar?"

The last time Annie was in a bar it didn't turn out too good. "My place. I'm heading home now." She pulled out of the parking lot and pointed her car in the direction of her house. "I'll order a pizza and I do believe I have several bottles of wine. If you want anything stronger, feel free to bring it."

"Wine will do. No anchovies on the pizza."

"Yeah. Yeah. I remember. See you soon." She pressed the button on her Bluetooth to end the call.

The pizza and Terry arrived at the same time. Terry was tipping the driver when Annie opened the door. "I would have taken care of that," Annie said.

"And now you don't have to." Terry handed the pizza box to Annie and followed her inside.

"I thought we could eat this on the deck. It's a beautiful day and I don't get fresh air too often."

"Lead the way."

"Glasses and wine on the kitchen table. Grab them, please." Annie took a couple of plates from the cupboard and napkins from the counter.

"What's new on the Nicole front?" Terry helped herself to a slice of pizza while Annie poured the wine.

"The Nicole front?"

"You know what I mean. I watched your show. Those are two gorgeous women. If that is the lesbian pool you get to choose from, I might be willing to jump ship and switch teams."

Annie laughed. "Liar. You like man bits too much. But you're right. They are both beautiful."

"They seem to be getting along well. Maybe too well? Are there any signs of which way this is going to end?"

Annie hesitated. No one was supposed to know the ending of the show. But Terry could be trusted. "We've filmed the final episode. The final interview really. The one where their decision is revealed." She took a long swig of her wine and let it roll around in her mouth as she watched Terry.

"You're an asshole. You know that? Are you going to tell me or just stare at me while you drink wine?"

"What was the question again?"

"What did they decide? Are they staying together or not?"

"Not."

Terry sat up straight. "What? They broke up?"

"You can't tell anyone. It needs to stay under wraps until the finale."

"So, I should cancel my interview with the six o'clock news?"

"You should." Annie dragged a piece of pizza from the box to her plate. She pulled a loose piece of cheese from the edge and popped it into her mouth.

"I would imagine that was quite a relief."

Annie shook her head. "It was kind of confusing. I mean, like you said, they seemed to be getting along so well. But at the same time, I was glad. And sad. For Nicole. And Lisa. But they seem okay. Nicole has been—I don't know—distant, since…" She felt like she was rambling. Letting all her thoughts out at once.

"Since what? What happened?"

"We had—I'm not sure how to explain it. An awkward moment." Annie told her what had happened.

"You almost kissed her?"

"Yeah. I guess that would sum it up. And she has pretty much been avoiding me ever since." Annie took a bite of her pizza. It felt good to share some of the thoughts that had been swirling through her head the last few weeks.

"Do you think it's a lost cause?"

"I hope not. But I don't know. I don't know what to think anymore."

"I still say go for it. What's the worst that can happen?" Terry sipped her wine.

"I get punched in the face and she quits."

"Yeah. I guess that would be pretty bad. Do you really think that can happen?"

Annie tilted her head back and watched a cloud go by for a few long moments before answering. "Not the punching part, but she could quit. I don't want that."

"You're willing to let go of the possibility of being with her because you're afraid of losing an employee? That doesn't make much sense."

"Nicole is much more than an employee."

Terry dropped her pizza onto her plate and folded her hands. "That's the point. She means more to you than that. You need to let her know how you feel. If you lose her because of that she wasn't meant for you. But if you don't tell her you are going to regret it. Annie, don't let this one get away."

"It's like that saying. If you love something, set it free."

"Hell no. I'm saying don't set her free. Tie her up, make her listen to you. Show her how much you care."

Annie couldn't help but laugh. "I don't know if tying her up is the best idea."

"You don't know. Sounds kinky to me. She might like it. The point is, *tell* her. If you don't, someone else is going to snatch her up. Just wait and see." She paused. "No. Don't wait and see. Don't wait."

"She just broke up with her wife. Don't you think that would be a little insensitive on my part?"

"Come on. It's not like it was a real marriage. They did things backwards. There was no love involved. Does she seem brokenhearted?"

Annie didn't even have to think about that one. "No."

"Then if I were you, I wouldn't wait too long. This kind of thing doesn't come around too often." She tapped her chest. "Listen to your heart for a change instead of your head. Annie, don't let the chance for love slip through your fingers."

"What if she doesn't feel the same?"

"Then at least you know you tried. But, Annie, what if she does?"

Annie was afraid to hold onto that thought. Afraid to open herself up. To be vulnerable.

"It takes strength to be vulnerable you know?" Terry said.

"Get out of my head."

"Why? It's so warm and squishy in there."

"You're in rare form today."

"Me? I'm always in this form. It's your form we're talking about. You need to change things up. If you keep doing what you've been doing, you'll keep getting what you've been getting. And ending up alone."

"What's wrong with being alone?"

"Nothing if that's what you really want. But I know what you really want is Nicole. I'm not sure how many other ways I can say this to get through to you." She took a bite of her pizza and washed it down with wine.

"You don't need to say it any other way. When the time is right, I'll tell her."

"And when will that be?"

"I don't know. But I will when it's time."

That answer seemed to satisfy Terry. At least for the moment. Yes. She would tell Nicole how she felt about her when the time was right. She needed to let her have some peace after Lisa and the marriage. Then she would tell her. She could do that. She hoped.

Chapter Thirteen

"I got a call from *Entertainment Tonight*," Annie said to Nicole the next day as they rode up to the office together in the elevator. It was rare for them to both arrive at the office at the same time.

"Yeah. About that..." Nicole had failed to mention it to Annie. She hoped they would have just dropped it. But reality TV was all the rage these days so she could see why they didn't.

"I know they called you first for an interview. You did the right thing referring them to me. This kind of stuff should come through me anyway."

"I have no idea how they got my number," Nicole said.

"It only takes a few bucks and the right website and you can find out just about anything thanks to the internet. Do you know if they called Lisa?"

Nicole didn't.

"I'll give her a call later. How would you feel about doing an interview?"

"Not crazy about the idea. Lisa would be much better at it if she wants to do it."

"They were hoping to get both of you together. We can talk about it later. The reporter is coming by in a little while to discuss it. So, you should probably stay in your office while he's here."

"Fine with me. I'm not big into this celebrity thing. Sorry."

The elevator doors opened, and Annie waited to let Nicole exit first. "No need to be sorry. But these interviews are important." She stopped walking.

Nicole took two more steps and turned around.

"Nicole, I know you didn't want the attention—"

"And what about what I do want to do?"

"I don't follow."

Nicole took the two steps it took to reach Annie. She stopped thinking and let her heart take over. She took Annie's face in both her hands and kissed her. Hard.

Nicole's blood rushed to her center as the kiss deepened. She was tired of waiting. Waiting for the right moment. Waiting for Annie to confess her feelings. Waiting to feel what it was like to possess Annie's mouth. Her delicious, warm, soft mouth.

Nicole's arms pressed against the closed elevator doors on each side of Annie as her mouth pressed against hers. She moved closer pressing her body into Annie's. Annie opened her mouth enough to let Nicole's insistent tongue in to search out her own.

Was that ding in Nicole's ears coming from her heart? Or was it—the elevator doors opened behind Annie, and she stumbled backward. Nicole's arms went around her trying to stop her from falling.

A pair of hands, directly behind Annie stopped them from tumbling into the elevator.

"Hey, boss," Lace said. "Nicole. Fancy meeting you here."

Somewhere along the line, the kiss had stopped and been replaced with them fighting to remain upright. Nicole got her footing and pulled Annie to her. It took her a moment to realize what had just happened.

"Umm…" Annie said. "We were just…"

"I saw what you were just," Lace said. "And it's about time."

"What?" Annie asked.

"I've felt the sexual tension between the two of you forever. It's about time you did something about it."

All this time, Nicole thought she'd covered it well. Guess not.

The elevator doors closed again and started moving downward. Nicole let go of Annie and took a step to the side. The elevator opened on the first floor and three people got on.

The blood was starting to return to Nicole's extremities and embarrassment made her flush hot. How had a moment that was so perfect gone so wrong, so fast? Fingers entwined with hers and she looked down to see Annie's hand in hers. She looked up into Annie's eyes. A smile spread across her face.

Back up on the third floor, Lace, Nicole, and Annie exited the elevator and made their way to their offices. Annie's hand was still warm in Nicole's.

"I'll just..." Lace said. She slipped into her own office and shut the door.

"Your office or mine?" Nicole asked. "I'd like to finish what I started. That is if you want to."

"Why wait that long?" Annie closed the gap between them and kissed Nicole. Thoroughly. Completely. Leaving her breathless.

"Excuse me." They had been so caught up with each other that they hadn't noticed a man standing there. How long had he been there? "I'm looking for Annie Jackson. Can you tell me if I'm in the right place?"

Annie straightened her shirt that had somehow become disheveled in their moment of passion. "I'm Annie."

Nicole pulled Annie's shirt down in the back, an act almost as intimate as the kiss they'd just shared. She hoped Annie didn't mind, but Annie didn't seem to notice.

He put his hand out. "I'm Jeff Miller. We spoke on the phone. I'm from *Entertainment Tonight*. I'm a little early."

Oh fuck.

"I'm…a…just…umm…gonna go to my office," Nicole said and turned to go.

"Your office? You're Nicole. Right? You work here? Does Lisa work here too?" He turned to Annie. "Is this whole show a scam? Faked?"

Double fuck.

"No. It's not fake. Why don't we step into my office and I'll explain everything, Mr. Miller."

Nicole started to follow them, thought better of it, went to her own office, and closed the door. What had she just done? She'd waited so long to act on her feelings for Annie. Why couldn't she have waited a little longer? And to make it even worse, that guy now knew she worked for Annie. She'd messed everything up. Annie might never forgive her for this. And she wouldn't blame her. Bile rose in her throat.

"Please, have a seat, Mr. Miller." Annie gestured to the chair in front of the desk.

"It's Jeff." He pulled his phone from his jacket pocket, pressed something on the screen a few times and set it on the desk in front of him.

Annie could see it was recording their conversation. "I'm going to have to ask you to turn that off. I'll tell you what's going on, but some of this needs to be off the record." She sat in her chair and waited.

"You tell me what part is off the record and I'll stop recording then. I don't want you to say you were misquoted, and this makes sure that doesn't happen."

Annie blew out a breath. How was she going to fix this? She couldn't afford to lose this show and she sure as hell didn't want to lose Nicole. It had taken them forever to get this far and Nicole had taken the first step. The step Annie had been too afraid to take. Granted the timing could have been better, but she wouldn't change a thing. That thought surprised her. Her career had been everything to her, right up until the time Nicole kissed her and everything changed. Nicole now took priority.

Jeff tapped a finger on the desk, bringing Annie back to the present moment.

"Nicole does work for me. She's the computer programmer."

"What exactly is her job?" Jeff asked.

Annie explained what Nicole did and how she had come to be one of the brides. "Now the next part is off the record. Please stop the recording."

Jeff did as Annie asked. "I'm not going to promise that I won't include anything you are about to say. This is a story people are going to want to hear. You're obviously having an affair with one of your brides."

Annie shook her head. "We aren't having an affair. What you witnessed was the first time anything physical transpired between us. I'll admit there have been feelings, but Nicole was married. The marriage to Lisa was real and Nicole didn't do anything inappropriate."

"So, the marriage is over now?"

"Please don't report that. The success of the show depends on keeping the viewers wondering how it all turns out."

"Looks like it turned out pretty good for you."

Annie ignored the comment. "Lisa doesn't know anything about this. She thinks Nicole was an applicant just like she was. She doesn't deserve to be hurt by any of this."

"Our intention isn't to hurt anyone, but this is news. I need to report it. I won't reveal the final decision the brides make." He paused. "But I *am* going to report the kiss."

"Please don't do that." Annie wasn't beyond begging.

"Tell you what, we normally report a story as soon as we have it. We like to keep things fresh and up-to-date. We'll hold off until tomorrow. That gives you a day to do damage control. If you can. That's the best I can do."

"Please," Annie said again.

"I can't sit on this. You have a show to run and so do we. If we don't do it, someone else will get wind of this and run it. This kind of thing doesn't stay quiet for long. We are all about scooping the other guy. Anything else you want to add before I go?"

"I take full responsibility for it. Nicole and Lisa were totally innocent."

"Got it. Story runs at seven tomorrow evening." He stood, pulled a business card from his wallet, and set it on the desk. "Call if there is anything else you would like to add. Have a good day." He made his way out of the office.

"Have a good day?" Annie repeated once he was gone. "Started out that way and now I'm having a fucked day. Fuck. Fuck. Fuck."

She gave him time to make his way to the elevator and out of the building before knocking on Lace's and Nicole's doors. "Meeting in my office. Now."

"I am so sorry, Annie," Nicole started. "I never should have—"

"No. Stop. Don't apologize for kissing me. I wouldn't change a thing about that. Not crazy that the witness to it is a reporter for *Entertainment Tonight*. But there is nothing we can do about that now. He's going to run the story tomorrow evening. Any suggestions on how we can control the fallout?"

"A reporter saw you two kissing?" Lace asked.

"Yeah. I need to tell Lisa before she finds out somewhere else," Nicole said.

"Yes. Of course," Annie said. "Right now, it's his word against ours. Should we deny it?"

"No," Lace said. "We use it to our advantage."

"And how do we do that?" Annie asked.

"I haven't figured that out yet. But I will."

"Okay. You get to work on that. Nicole, go talk to Lisa. I'm going to—I don't know what. But whatever it is I want to talk to Nicole alone for a minute, Lace."

"You got it, boss. Going to work on a solution."

Annie waited until she heard Lace's door close. "Come here," she said to Nicole.

Nicole closed the short distance between them in three steps. "Yes."

Annie wrapped her arms around her. "Thank you."

"For what?"

"For kissing me. I've wanted to do that for months now."

"Why didn't you?"

"You were married. It wouldn't have been right. I suspect it was the same reason you didn't do it before today."

"There was a little thing called integrity that got in the way."

"I'm glad you have integrity. I'm glad you decided not to stay with Lisa. And I'm glad you have such kissable lips and you decided to plant them on me."

"Even if it means the end of the show?"

Annie shook her head. "It's just a little setback. Not the end of the world and not the end of the show. I won't let it be." She pulled Nicole to her and kissed her. She'd thought about moments like this but had never dreamed it would be as good as it truly was. She'd read about kissing that caused your toes to curl. Until this moment she didn't believe it was true. But that's exactly what Nicole's kiss was doing to her. Among other things that she couldn't think about now. There would be plenty of time for that. Reluctantly, Annie pulled her mouth away from Nicole's. "You need to get going. Lisa should hear this from you."

"Lisa. Yes." She kissed Annie softly on the lips and wiggled out of her embrace. It was all Annie could do not to pull her back in.

"Let me know how it goes and if there is anything I can do to help."

"You got it. I'll call you later."

"Thanks, Nicole."

Annie sat at her desk and lowered her face into her hands. How could one day hold so much promise and yet so much dread?

❖

Nicole drove to Lisa's house. She took her time explaining to Lisa how she came to be bride number two. Lisa sat without saying anything. "I was a match. That part wasn't faked. And, Lisa, I tried. When I saw you standing there in your white dress, looking beautiful, I vowed to do whatever I could to make this work."

"Why are you telling me this now?" Lisa sat at the kitchen table, an untouched cup of tea in front of her.

"I had every intention of telling you this when it was all over. After the show aired, I guess. I never wanted to deceive you. But something else happened." She hesitated, not sure how to say the rest.

"What?" Lisa asked. "Just say it."

"I kissed Annie and a reporter from *Entertainment Tonight* saw it."

"What? Why? How?"

"As much as I wanted the marriage to work, I realized that while my feelings for you weren't developing, they were developing for Annie."

Lisa shook her head. "We didn't stand a chance, did we?"

"I wanted us to. I couldn't force my feelings for you to grow and I couldn't stop them from growing for Annie. I even avoided her for a while, trying to make them go away. It didn't help."

"Were you two carrying on behind my back the whole time?"

Nicole reached across the table and took both of Lisa's hands in hers. To her surprise, Lisa didn't pull away. "No. Nothing happened until today. I wanted to honor our marriage. I know we aren't legally divorced yet, but we are separated. I guess, I thought it would be okay."

Lisa sat quietly, not saying anything for a long while.

"What are you thinking?"

"I don't know what to think. Did Annie plant that note to get us to fight so she could have you?"

Nicole hadn't thought of that. "No. I don't think so. She was trying to create drama for the show."

"For her it was all about the show. It didn't matter that she was playing with people's lives?"

"It wasn't like that. Exactly. She wanted to give you the best match she could. That was me. I never meant to have my data used. I put it in to test the program. But Annie didn't want to settle for the closest match after me. Because she wasn't a match at all. She wasn't what you wanted in a wife. Not even close. If nothing else, give Annie credit for trying to give you the best match."

"Go back to the *Entertainment Tonight* guy. You said he saw you kissing. That can't be good."

"It's not. He's going to run the story tomorrow evening. I don't know for sure what he's going to say." And the possibilities made Nicole's stomach turn sour.

"I'm going to be a laughingstock."

"No, you aren't. You'll look like the unwitting wife. I'll look like the asshole, and Annie, well, who knows how it will paint her. But I'm sure it won't be good."

"You'll forgive me if I don't feel sorry for her. And you. I expected more from you."

"I couldn't tell you. This marriage wouldn't have worked if you knew I worked for Annie and was actually second choice."

"This marriage didn't work anyway." She pulled her hands away.

"Good point." Nicole wasn't sure she was explaining things very well. "It wasn't anyone's fault. I tried. You tried. And Annie never got in the way."

"Your feelings for her did."

"I don't think they did. With or without Annie in the picture my feelings for you were more like a friend. Like a sister. There was no changing that. As much as I tried. Do you think you can ever forgive me?"

Lisa took a deep breath. Nicole couldn't read her expression. She didn't want Lisa to hate her, even though she had every right to.

"This is a lot to digest. You need to give me time."

Nicole nodded. "I am sorry. I never meant to hurt you."

As soon as she left Lisa's, Nicole called her parents and brother and sister-in-law to give them a heads-up. "Best not to answer any questions if you get a phone call," she told them. Having any of them try to defend her could cause more harm than good. She had a feeling the harm was already done. There was nothing to do but wait for the fallout.

Chapter Fourteen

I thought wine might help us get through this," Annie said to Nicole as she handed her a glass.

"Thanks. Do you have any idea what to expect?" Nicole asked.

"Not a clue. I tried to call in some favors to get some information, but no one seemed to have anything to share."

Nicole sat on the couch and leaned back. She'd never been to Annie's house before. Under different circumstances she might have been given a tour instead of ushered in, handed a glass of wine, and asked to sit.

Lace was already there when Nicole arrived.

To say the house was under decorated was an accurate assessment. The only personal item was a picture of Annie and a woman Nicole assumed was her sister, in a frame on top of the small bookcase. Most of the books were about succeeding in business or how to write a screenplay.

"I didn't know you wanted to write a screenplay," Nicole said.

"I gave up on that a long time ago. Maybe that's why I chose to do a reality show. Very little scripting involved."

"Just enough to make things interesting." Nicole sipped her wine.

"Things got interesting on their own. No scripting involved in this one."

"But scripting may be what gets us out of this mess," Lace said. Her pink hair now had a streak of purple running through it, just the latest in a long list of hair changes.

"What do you mean?" Annie stopped her pacing and sat on the other end of the couch, across from the chair Lace occupied.

"We take whatever is reported on *Entertainment Tonight* and use it to our advantage. We create our own commercial promo. Is it true? Can Nicole and Lisa get past the rumors and find happiness in each other? Does the showrunner cause problems for the new couple? That kind of thing."

"That could work," Annie said. "Although I'm not sure we should drag me into it."

"Depending on what they say about you and Nicole kissing, we may have to."

Nicole watched the exchange without contributing to it. Lace's idea was a good one. It would bring even more attention to Nicole, which she didn't want, but knew she couldn't avoid.

Annie grabbed the remote from the coffee table and turned on the television. They sat through way too many commercials waiting for *Entertainment Tonight* to start. They started the show with the usual teasers. Who was Angelina seen out with? What kind of trouble was brewing on the set of Tom's new movie? Who was Nicole Hart from the new reality show, *I Do, I Don't* seen kissing that wasn't her wife? Damn. So far, not so good.

Nicole drained her glass of wine and refilled it as they waited for the hammer to drop. It was the last story of the night, giving it an air of importance. They started with footage of Annie and Nicole walking into the office building together. What the hell? Jeff must have taken it with his cell phone before he entered the building. It was slightly blurry, suggesting that it had been taken from quite a distance away and then blown up. Bet he was sorry he didn't have his phone recording video when he rounded the corner to the hallway where he caught Annie and Nicole kissing.

"Nicole Hart, star of the new reality show, *I Do, I Don't* was seen by this reporter, kissing Annie Jackson, show runner. Nicole's wife, Lisa, was nowhere in sight. We've reached out to her but so far have no comment. We've also learned that not only is Ms. Hart one of the brides who marries a stranger when they meet for the first time at the altar, she is also employed by Annie Jackson as her main computer programmer." At least the picture they showed of Nicole was flattering. Annie's, not so much. It was a ploy to paint her as a villain.

"It begs the question," the report continued, "is this show on the up-and-up or was all of it faked from the start? Annie Jackson assured me that it was real. The match. The marriage. The effort to make it work. But can her word be trusted? She obviously can't be trusted alone with one of the brides. We'll bring you more on this story as we work to uncover the truth."

Annie clicked the TV off. "Well?"

"I'll get to work on the promos for this right away," Lace said. "We've got this. If nothing else, they just gave us a whole lot of free publicity."

"If nothing else?" Annie asked. "That's what I'm worried about. They didn't make me look too good." Not that that was what she was really worried about. She was worried about what Nicole had to go through and the unwanted attention she would more than likely get.

Nicole moved closer and took her hand. "You've got this. Lace is right. It's free publicity. And like a bad kidney stone, this will pass."

Annie laughed. "Yes, but like a kidney stone, it's going to hurt like hell."

"Trust me on this," Lace said. "This is going to work out. I'm going to the office to get started. I'll put together some YouTube clips, TV promos, TikTok videos, you name it."

"That can wait till morning," Annie said.

"No. I wouldn't be able to sleep tonight anyway. Too many ideas." Lace set her half-empty glass of wine on the coffee table and headed to the door. She stopped, hand on the doorknob and turned back. "Please don't worry. We'll turn this around." With that, she made her exit.

Annie and Nicole were alone. All Annie wanted to do was scoop Nicole up in her arms and take her to the bedroom. But that probably wasn't the best idea. At least not right now. But a long make out session might work. Annie shook her head. *Stop. Now is not the time.* Too much to deal with.

Apparently, Nicole thought now was the perfect time. She straddled Annie on the couch and planted a kiss on her forehead and cheek before seeking out her mouth. Annie melted under Nicole's warm, soft lips. She slipped her hands under Nicole's shirt and ran her hands up her back, sliding her fingertips across satiny smooth skin. The sensation brought a surge of wetness, and she clenched her legs against the sensation. The move only added to the building pressure.

As quickly as she started, Nicole stopped the kiss but held onto Annie's face. "I should get going. If I don't…" She paused. "If I don't," she started again. "I can't be held responsible for what happens. And I think it's too soon to happen. Don't you think it's too soon to happen? Yeah," Nicole continued, before Annie had a chance to answer. "Too soon." She slipped off Annie's lap.

Annie had trouble catching her breath. "How can you even talk after that. So intense," she managed to squeak out.

"Just talented I guess." Nicole's smile lit up her face. Her eyes sparkled, even in the dim light cast by the lamp in the corner. "But I really am going to go. This has been quite a week."

Annie couldn't argue with that. "It has. You should go home and get some sleep. We have a lot to do tomorrow." Although

Annie was sure that if Nicole was feeling any of the same things she was, neither one of them was going to get much sleep.

She gave Nicole a good night kiss at the door and watched as she walked to her car and drove away. She was still standing there long after the car was out of sight. The October air had a chill to it and she wrapped her arms around herself against it.

Her phone somewhere in the house rang and she went in search of it. She found it on the coffee table next to the almost empty bottle of wine. She didn't recognize the number. "Hello?"

"Annie Jackson?"

"Yes."

"Hello, Ms. Jackson. My name is Jennifer Tomlin. I'm calling from *Good Morning America*. I'd like to set up an on-air interview with you, Nicole Hart, and Lisa Morgan. Robin Roberts personally requested this. She would be the one conducting the interview."

Annie's head was spinning. She was hoping to get national interviews for the show to promote it, but up until now her requests had fallen on deaf ears. Maybe Lace was right. The publicity might just do the show some good.

"Ms. Jackson?"

"Umm. Yes. I'm here. I'm sure we can set something up. I'll have to get in touch with Lisa and Nicole."

"Of course. Let me give you my direct number. If you could give me a call back in the next day or two, that would be great."

Three more phone calls followed. Each one requesting an interview for a national talk show. Annie gave them all the same answer.

She was prepared to do the interviews. She hoped Nicole and Lisa would agree as well. How many more things could she ask Nicole to do before Nicole started to resent her?

❖

The interview with *Good Morning America* was set up virtually, so they didn't have to drive to New York City. Annie was in her office, while Nicole was at Lisa's house, so they were seen together. It wasn't exactly honest, but it was necessary for the sake of the show. Nicole could feel the tension when Lisa took her hand and forced a smile.

"We're set to start in two minutes," Jennifer said. "Ms. Roberts is standing by. Any questions?" The split screen had Annie on one side and Nicole and Lisa on the other. It switched to just Jennifer whenever she spoke.

The show had provided makeup artists, camera men, lights, and boom mics. Lisa's small living room seemed super crowded. Nicole imagined Annie's office probably felt the same.

"And we go live in five, four, three…" Jennifer went silent and her face was replaced by Robin Roberts's.

She started by asking Annie questions about the original idea for the show, how she went about choosing the brides and how she managed when the second bride backed out.

"So, at that point you had no choice but to recruit your own employee, Nicole Hart?"

"Yes. She was the next closest match. She hadn't met Lisa, so it still fit in with the spirit of the show."

"Let's hear from the brides themselves, Nicole Hart and Lisa Morgan." The red light on the camera in front of them lit up and their faces filled the monitor. "Ladies, it's good to have you here. I'm curious, what makes someone willing to marry a total stranger? Lisa, let's start with you."

Nicole squeezed her hand, grateful that she didn't have to talk first.

"The simple answer is love. I was hoping to find my person. I've never been into the bar scene and the dating sites didn't yield anyone that I could connect with. So why not trust a computer program to find the perfect match for me?"

"I won't ask you how that worked out for you. I see Nicole sitting next to you, holding your hand. It looks like you two are pretty cozy. But there are rumors that Nicole was seen kissing someone else. Can you tell me how that affected you?"

"Rumors can only hurt you if you believe them," Lisa said. How could she keep her cool and answer so calmly? She was so good at this.

"Nicole, I understand you work for the production company that makes the reality show. Is it ethical for you to do that *and* be a bride? Isn't that a conflict of interest?"

"Not at all. We followed the rules and heart of the show. I hadn't met Lisa and didn't know anything about her. I was a match according to the computer algorithm."

Robin continued asking questions, jumping from one to the other. She was thoughtful and kind, for which Nicole was very grateful. They wrapped it up and it was over almost as quickly as it had started.

"Thank you for agreeing to do this," Nicole said to Lisa once everyone from the *Good Morning America* crew left.

"I don't want the show to fail. How selfish would that be of me? Just because I didn't find my person doesn't mean the next brides won't. I think it's a worthy show with a noble cause."

"I appreciate that. Lisa, I don't want you to hate me."

"I could never hate you. I just feel…" she trailed off, obviously trying to get her thoughts together. "Left out. Like everyone knew the punchline to a joke but me."

"This wasn't a joke, to me or to Annie."

"I know that. It feels kind of crappy to have the whole world know that I had the wool pulled over my eyes."

Nicole smiled, trying to lighten the mood. "I don't think it's the whole world, probably not more than North America and Puerto Rico." Nicole was relieved to see Lisa return the smile.

"Oh, that makes me feel much better."

"Aren't you the one who told me we will be yesterday's news soon? Destined to be replaced by a new set of brides in a few months."

"Oh yeah. That *was* me. I'm pretty smart, aren't I?"

"Smart, beautiful, kind, sexy in a sisterly kind of way," Nicole said.

"Oh, that's gross." Lisa laughed.

Nicole joined in. "It is, isn't it. Sorry."

"I think I just threw up a little in my mouth."

"Now, that's gross." It was good to laugh with Lisa again.

One down, three more interviews to go. Nicole hoped they all went as smoothly.

The ratings doubled when the third episode aired and went up again for the fourth. Lace had been right. The publicity was helping. The website was blowing up with applicants from all over the country wanting to take a chance on love with a stranger. Annie couldn't have been more pleased.

She finished editing the last episode. It was both a triumph and a letdown. It wasn't that she didn't have plenty to do to get ready for the next season. She didn't have kids, but she thought maybe this was the feeling a parent had when they sent their child off to college and into the world and they were no longer there to protect them.

Annie looked up when Nicole knocked on her door. "Hey there. Come on in. I just put the final episode to bed. We should get Lace in here and open a bottle of champagne." She rolled her chair back to her mini fridge and pulled out a bottle. "And just by coincidence I happen to have a bottle right here."

"That *is* quite the coincidence," Nicole said. "And look, there are three plastic champagne flutes right there on your desk. Can you believe our luck?"

"I can. Because I have the best team ever. Every single one of you went above and beyond for this show."

"I know Sandy did," Nicole said with a chuckle. "There were a few times I had to stop her from following me into the bathroom."

"Now that's dedication." Annie called Lace on her phone and asked her to join them.

"We are celebrating." Annie uncorked the bottle sending the stopper flying across the room, despite her efforts to keep it corralled in the dish towel she'd brought. The towel did manage to catch the foam that splashed out and cascaded over the side. She poured three glasses, handed them out, and held hers up. "To the newest surprise hit of the season, *I Do, I Don't*, and making our reality show a—well—a reality. I couldn't have done it without you."

"And to a great boss," Lace added.

"I'll drink to that." Nicole took a sip. "Great job, by the way, Lace." "I've seen some of your video clips on TikTok. They really make the show look intriguing. I would watch it if I wasn't in it. And if I liked reality shows."

Annie's glass was halfway to her mouth when she stopped and searched Nicole's face, trying to decide if she was joking. "You don't like reality shows?"

"I mean, I like ours. Ours is good."

"But in general, you don't?" Annie tried to hide the disappointment from her voice. She wasn't sure if she was successful.

"I guess I don't see the point in having your life recorded for other people to watch. Our show at least has a reason for being. An end goal if you will."

All these months and Annie had no idea Nicole felt this way. She wondered what else she didn't know about her.

"Don't go by me. These shows get good ratings, so obviously other people love them."

"You knew this was a reality show when you applied. How come you wanted this job?"

"I love designing computer programs."

Annie shook her head. "So, you didn't like reality shows and you didn't believe in love when you started here? How do you feel now?"

"True. I had given up on ever finding love. And now. Well, now I have a great friend in Lisa, so the reality show stepped up my reality and I do believe in the possibility of being happy with someone. I don't want to mention any names here." She grinned.

The fact that she didn't actually say she believed in love didn't escape Annie's notice. Annie didn't want to push the questions any further, afraid of what the answers would be.

"Hey," Lace said. "We've all grown working on this show. I know I have."

Annie felt like she had too.

"What do you have going the rest of the day?" Nicole asked. "Now that you're done editing."

"I was thinking lunch outside at the park if you would like to join me." Annie thought she should probably invite Lace too, so she didn't appear rude.

"I can't," Lace said, as if reading her mind. "Lots to do. But you two go ahead. Enjoy yourselves. In fact…" She stood. "I'm going to get back to work now." She held up her nearly full glass. "And I'm taking this with me." She trotted off to her own office, waving behind her as she went out the door.

"I would love to have lunch with you. Do you think it's safe? I mean who knows what reporters are lurking around trying to get pictures or a story."

"Good point." Annie should have thought of that herself. "How about dinner, then? My place around seven?"

"Sure. What can I bring?"

"Just your smiling face." Annie leaned back in her chair. "I'm going to go through the list of new applicants and narrow down the choices for our first bride." Annie had access to each applicant's full information, name, and picture. Nicole only had access to the data she needed to enter for each one and their assigned code number. "I can't believe how many new applications have come in." She would have a much wider pool of women to choose from than she'd had for season one. She hadn't received official word yet but had it on good authority that they were getting picked up for a second season.

"Whatever you do, don't pick me again. I'm through marrying strangers." Although being married to Lisa had given her valuable insights to improve the questions on the application and ways to tweak the algorithm to make it more reliable and insure better matches.

"You've got nothing to worry about. I'm through handing you over to other women. I'd like to keep you all to myself for a while." They'd done a whole lot of kissing but hadn't talked about what any of it meant or where they wanted it to go. Annie hoped she hadn't overstepped.

"I would like that, too." Nicole said.

Nicole was on the same page. That was a good thing. And she was coming over for dinner. Annie couldn't remember the last time she'd cooked for a guest. It was probably her sister, several months before she started working on the show. Her personal life had taken a back seat to just about everything else, especially her career. She'd let her few friends fall by the wayside as she climbed the ladder giving everything she had to her job. It was time for that to change. Tonight, Nicole. Next week, maybe a dinner party with Nicole, Terry, and a few of those forgotten friends—if she hadn't lost them altogether.

"I should get back to work. I'm refining the algorithm to include more personality traits. I'm bound and determined to find the perfect match."

I think I already have, Annie thought, taking in the beautiful woman standing across from her. "I appreciate your dedication. Just think about it, Nicole. We could be changing people's lives forever and for the better."

"I hadn't really thought about it that way. What power."

"You know what they say. With great power comes great algorithms."

"I'm pretty sure that's not how the saying goes, but close enough. I'm out of here. If I don't see you before we leave, I'll see you tonight for dinner. Bringing nothing but my smiling face." She faked a wide grin, making Annie laugh, and exited to her own office.

Annie pulled up the pictures of the new applicants and scrolled through them, marking any that she wanted to investigate further. She wanted someone completely different looking than Lisa. Not that Lisa wasn't the ideal bride. She was. But Annie wanted the second season to have a different look than the first.

She had the large list narrowed down to ten women, each beautiful, in their own right. Six blondes, three redheads, and one with short dark hair, highlighted with streaks of lighter brown. She printed their bios, questionnaires, and photos and gave each one their own folder labeled with only their code numbers. She'd planned to go over each one in depth, trimming it down to the top three and then setting up in-person interviews with each one. Beauty only took you so far, even on a reality show. There needed to be substance underneath it. Beauty, brains, wit, and a winning personality was called for. Once they had the first bride, it was up to Nicole to run her magic program and find her the best match. This time, however, they would have a backup plan in place in case one of the brides pulled out.

She called Lace to her office and handed her the files. "Can you go through these and see if there are any red flags I missed? We'll run complete background checks once we narrow the field down more."

"You got it, boss."

"I'm heading home. Nicole's coming over so I've got a dinner to make—or order. I haven't decided yet." She hadn't cooked in so long she wasn't sure she could do it anymore. Besides, she was pretty sure the only thing she had in the house were a few packages of microwave popcorn and a jar of peanut butter.

"Pizza's always a good choice."

"I need something much fancier than pizza. I think this will be our first official date. I want this to be special."

"Maybe add cheesy breadsticks?" Lace said with a smirk.

"I know. I know. Go back to work, Lace. I'm going. I'm going."

As soon as she got home, Annie ordered food to be delivered a little before seven. Not that she didn't want Nicole to know she'd ordered dinner. She just wanted to make sure she had the food ready when she got there.

She set the table with the good china, which was anything other than paper plates, and happened to find two tapered candles in the junk drawer. She lit one and let the melting wax drip onto a plate and stuck the candle in it, so it stood upright and did the same with the second candle. It would have to do. She made a mental note to pick up some nice things for their next romantic dinner. Annie hoped this would be the first of many.

Somewhere she had cloth napkins. That would be so much nicer than using folded paper towels. Damn. She should have planned this better, given herself more time. The food arrived right on time and Annie set it on the table, still covered.

At seven fifteen, Annie blew out the candles and wondered if she should text Nicole to find out if she was still coming. A moment of panic caused a surge of acid in her stomach. What if Nicole changed her mind about this whole thing? It took several minutes to talk herself down from the ledge. *She's late, not running off to Tahiti with some stranger.* Now why would her brain go there? Stop. Other than the success of her show, she hadn't wanted anything this much in a very long time. In fact, she couldn't remember the last time she had all these feelings swirling around taking up so much space in her head and her heart.

The acid in her gut turned to excitement when the doorbell rang. She smoothed out her shirt, checked her face in the mirror in the hall, and made her way to the door. She felt her face drop when she opened it and found a strange man standing there. He had his phone in his outstretched hand. "I'm with the *Extra Showbiz*. Can I get a statement on the rumors that you are involved with one of the brides from your show, *I Do, I Don't*." There was another man holding a camera aimed at her a few feet down the driveway. *Please, Nicole, don't show up right now.*

She rattled off her phone number. "Call me at work tomorrow. Showing up at my home uninvited is not appropriate. Now I would appreciate it if you would leave."

"Speaking of inappropriate behavior, wouldn't you say that it was highly inappropriate of you and Nicole Hart, married to Lisa Morgan, to have an affair?"

Annie wondered if slamming the door in his face would help or hurt the show. At that moment, she didn't care. She slammed it and turned off the outside light. Not that it was that dark out, but she was trying to send a message. She let out a low growl. No wonder Nicole hated the attention. It felt so intrusive.

By seven thirty she moved the food from the dining room to the kitchen counter. She heard a knock on the back door that was so quiet, she wasn't sure that's what she really heard. "I swear to God that if that's a reporter, I'm going to shoot them." The fact that she didn't have a gun might prove to be a problem. "I'll stab them, then."

She opened the door a crack, keeping her foot firmly planted to stop the door from being pushed open farther. "What the hell..." she started and realized it was Nicole standing there.

Her normally perfect hair was mussed, a couple of crumpled leaves stuck out of her long locks. A scratch marked her cheek bright red.

Annie pulled her in, closed the door, and locked it. "Are you all right?"

Nicole was obviously shaken. "I was being followed. I thought I lost them, but they were parked in your driveway when I doubled back. I parked one street over and came through the woods to get here."

"Holy shit, Nicole. I'm so sorry." She wrapped her arms around her. She was shaking. "What a bunch of assholes. I'm going to call the police."

"No." Nicole pulled out of her embrace. "That's only going to cause more attention."

"Come and sit down." She led her to the living room and Nicole sat on the couch. Annie closed the drapes on the bay window. The sheer curtains would have stopped anyone from having a clear view inside, but why take any chances? "I'll get you a drink. Do you want wine, or I can get you something stronger?"

"Stronger might be better." Nicole wasn't a heavy drinker, but she had been so spooked being followed like that she needed something to take the edge off her rampant nerves.

Annie disappeared into the kitchen and reappeared with a glass of amber liquid. The first sip burned Nicole's throat. Too strong. "What is this?" She held up the glass.

"Bourbon. It's the only thing I have besides beer and wine. Do you want something else? I can add ginger ale if it's too strong."

"Would you mind?" Nicole stood.

"Sit." Annie took the glass. "I'll get it."

She returned with two glasses and handed one to Nicole. "Try it now." She sat next to her on the couch.

Nicole sipped. The bubbles tickled her nose, but the drink was much more palatable. "Much better." By the third sip she could feel herself starting to relax. She let out a deep breath.

"I'm so sorry," Annie started. "This is all—"

"Not your fault," Nicole said. "You didn't do this. We didn't plan on this happening."

"I know, but I'm the one that—"

"Just stop. We'll get through this. In the meantime, we need to be careful. That's all." Nicole's cheek stung and she rubbed it. Her finger had a small amount of blood on it. "Guess a tree branch got me."

"Here," Annie said, disappearing once again, this time down a hallway. "Let me…" She dabbed at Nicole's face with a warm washcloth and applied what Nicole guessed was an antibiotic cream. "It's just a scratch. You won't be scarred for life. At least not by this. I can't promise you won't have PTSD from being followed."

"Thank you," Nicole said. "That was awful. I don't think I've ever been so scared in my life. I didn't know what they wanted or why they were following me."

"They were reporters after a story. Probably hoping to catch you coming here."

"I'm not sure how much more of this I can take."

Annie put her arm around Nicole's shoulders. "I'm so sorry."

They sat like that for what felt like a long time, Nicole comforted by the warmth of Annie's embrace.

"What can I do to help?" Annie said.

"I think a kiss might make me feel even better."

Annie chuckled. "You think so? Then I better play doctor and try to cure you." She took Nicole's glass, set it on the coffee table, and pulled Nicole closer. The kiss started off softly, but quickly deepened.

Oh, yes. That did help. Soft lips, hands on her back and in her hair, Annie's breasts pressing into her own, did wonders to help her forget what had transpired. What was it again? What had transpired? She couldn't remember.

Her fingers trembled as she moved them through Annie's hair and down to her neck. Her skin so soft, so silky, so desirable. Nicole yielded to Annie's insistent tongue, letting her in to explore.

Explore. That's what Nicole wanted to do to Annie. Explore every inch of her. She brought her hands down and back up under Annie's shirt. Annie's mouth released hers momentarily and she let out a low groan as she skimmed her hands over Annie's breasts, the material from Annie's bra separating them.

Annie recaptured her mouth and Nicole slipped the offending material up, granting her full access. Annie's nipples stood at full attention as Nicole ran her palms over them, gently squeezing the full flesh around them.

Annie tugged at the bottom of Nicole's shirt and Nicole lifted her arms to let Annie remove it, breaking the kiss for only a second or two.

Nicole's shirt landed on the floor, followed by her bra and Annie's shirt. Nicole found herself lying on her back with Annie on top of her and very little memory of how they got in that position. Not that Nicole was complaining. The sensations from Annie's thigh pressed between her legs were building at an alarming rate. Nicole was so close to the edge, but she didn't want her first orgasm with Annie to be with her pants still on. She wanted it to be with Annie's fingers inside her. Filling her up.

Nicole broke the kiss. "Wait," she managed to squeak out.

Annie pushed herself up with one hand on each side of Nicole. She was breathing almost as hard as Nicole was. "What?" Her thigh was still pressing hard between Nicole's legs.

Nicole wiggled herself away from it. "I want this," she said. "Believe me I do. But..." She paused, not sure how to explain what she wanted.

"Just say it," Annie said gently. "But what?"

"But I want us both naked. I want—"

"Naked can be arranged." Annie stood and put a hand out to Nicole. Nicole took it and Annie pulled her up. "I don't believe I've given you a full tour of my house. I would like to remedy that right now. Let's start with my bedroom." She led Nicole down the hall. "Right this way. Bathroom on the left." She waved the hand that wasn't in Nicole's. "And bedroom on the right." They stepped into the bedroom.

She pulled Nicole to her, reached between them, unbuttoned and then slowly unzipped Nicole's pants. Nicole sucked in a breath as Annie's hand slipped down, into her underwear and her fingers teased Nicole's swollen flesh. A rush of wetness greeted her.

Annie's free hand pulled at Nicole's pants and then underwear until they were down around her ankles and Nicole stepped out of them and kicked them free. She wasn't sure how much longer she could remain standing with all the blood rushing from her extremities to her center. "You're still dressed," she whispered.

"Easy fix." Annie tossed her bra on the foot of the bed and exited her pants and underwear just as fast. "Naked. Happy now?"

"Extremely." Nicole took a moment to take in the woman before her. "You are so beautiful," she said.

Annie walked Nicole backward toward the bed, gently pushed her onto it, and climbed on top of her. Nicole could feel Annie's heart so close, beating the same rhythm as her own.

Annie's tongue entered her mouth as Annie's fingers entered her. Nicole pressed her feet into the bed as she bucked her hips upward, matching Annie's strokes with her own movements.

Annie placed small kisses along Nicole's jawline, neck, and shoulders, circling her belly button. Moving downward until her mouth was on Nicole. Her fingers continued their steady movement as her tongue went to work.

Nicole's hips rose off the bed as an orgasm ripped through her. Her breath caught in her throat and lights seemed to flash behind her closed eyes. "Oh God, oh God," she repeated as the rest of the world fell away and there was only her and Annie and wonderful sensations Annie had caused.

"You don't have to call me God," Annie said once Nicole came down from the ride and Annie was curled up beside her. "Your Highness will do."

"A well-deserved title," Nicole responded. "Your Highness."

"Nicole," Annie said, seeming to turn serious for a moment. "I know it's kind of late to ask, but are you sure this is okay? I mean I'm still your boss and everything."

Nicole didn't even have to think about her answer. "Yes, I'm sure. And after what I'm about to do to you, you're going to want to give me a raise."

"Oh. Okay. I do base my raises on performance. Just don't tell any of the other computer programmers that work for me."

"I'm the only programmer you've got."

Annie pulled Nicole closer. "Then I guess we've got no problem."

"Nope. As long as this isn't a problem." Nicole slid one finger, then two inside Annie.

Annie spread her legs wider, allowing Nicole better access. "Umm," Annie groaned, through clenched teeth. "That is definitely not a problem."

"Oh good. How about this?" Nicole ran her thumb through Annie's folds, keeping up the steady rhythm of her fingers.

Annie nodded, and Nicole surmised she was having trouble speaking.

Nicole lowered her mouth and swept her tongue around Annie's nipple. It stood at full attention deepening Nicole's desire to possess every part of her. She took the nipple fully into her mouth. The moan that escaped from Annie urged her on and she pressed herself into Annie's hip to help relieve the pressure that was building once again inside her, as Annie's pleasure became her own. She wrapped one leg around Annie's and pulled her center even closer to Annie's leg.

The rhythm of her fingers was matched beat for beat with her hips rubbing her most sensitive part against Annie. Annie's breathing picked up speed and then stopped completely as her muscles tightened around Nicole's fingers and she let herself go over the edge and into the abyss. It only took a few more seconds for Nicole to join her. She slipped her fingers from Annie, rolled on top of her, and pressed her wetness into Annie's. They rode the last waves of their orgasms together.

"You are amazing," Nicole said when she was finally able to catch her breath.

"I was thinking the same thing about you. And you can forget about that raise."

Nicole raised up on her arms so she could look into Annie's eyes. "Not good enough?"

"Too good. I'm signing over the whole production company to you. Hell, I'm going to throw in my house and goldfish too."

Nicole laughed. "You have a goldfish?"

"No. Remind me to have Lace pick one up so I can give it to you."

Nicole settled back down on top of Annie. "I don't want any of those things. I just want you. Naked. Underneath me like this. Forever." Was it too early to talk about forever? Probably. But in that moment, Nicole didn't care. She would be perfectly content to stay like this for the rest of her life.

"I like that plan. But..."

"But what? Am I hurting you?" She started to slide off Annie, but Annie held her in place.

"No. I love the feeling of you—your body—your magnificent body on top of mine. But I do have dinner waiting for you. I'm sure it's cold by now, but that's why God invented microwaves. Steak and lobster."

"For real? Why didn't you lead with that?"

"And miss all this? No way. But I would be happy to warm it up for you." Annie attempted to squirm out from under Nicole. But Nicole held firm. "No?" Annie asked.

"Not yet. I need to kiss you more. You okay with that or is the hunger too strong?"

"The hunger is for *you*, silly."

Two orgasms later, they headed into the kitchen to heat up their dinner.

Annie wasn't kidding, steak, lobster, cheese biscuits, and mashed potatoes were piled high on plates and warmed in the microwave. Annie warmed the butter to melt it for dipping. The food was almost as good as the lovemaking had been. Almost. They put the leftovers in the fridge and headed back to the bedroom for round two. Or was it round three?

CHAPTER FIFTEEN

The ratings continued to go up. Annie couldn't believe they were already airing episode twelve. The second season was guaranteed. Bride number one for season two was booked. She would have to come up with a better code name.

"Here is the list you asked for." Nicole entered Annie's office. "Door was open, so I let myself in. Hope that's okay."

"You are allowed in any of my doors without knocking first." Heat rushed to Annie's face.

"I thought there was that little thing called consent." Nicole set the folder on Annie's desk.

"You have my consent. Anytime. Any place."

"I think I'm going to throw up." Lace made a puking up motion with her finger and an open mouth. Annie hadn't seen her come in. "I mean, I'm all for romance, but that is just taking it too far.

"Lace," Annie said. "Don't you have something to do?"

"I did it." She waved a few pieces of paper in the air. "The list of updated questions for the new brides after the wedding."

"Great work. We appear to be working like a well-oiled machine here," Annie said.

"I don't want to hear how well-oiled you two are," Lace said, making a quick getaway.

"What's with her?" Nicole pointed a thumb in the direction Lace exited.

"No idea. Oh. I forgot to tell you that I set up a couple more interviews with you and Lisa."

"No. No. No."

Annie stood up and came around the desk. "What do you mean no?"

"I mean I'm done doing interviews. Isn't it bad enough reporters stalk me and make my life difficult?" Nicole absently rubbed the scratch on her cheek, now nearly healed.

Annie took both Nicole's hands in hers. "But this is part of the deal, honey. It helps people find the show."

Nicole shook her head. "Not fair, playing the *honey* card." Nicole pulled her hands away and took a step back. "Annie, I'm serious. This isn't fair anymore. Not to me and certainly not to Lisa."

"What do you mean?"

"Us, Lisa and I doing interviews and pretending that everything is going great between us. For what? For ratings? I don't want to pretend anymore."

What the hell? The ratings were important. Nicole knew that. She looked at her trying to decide if she was serious. She was. "Yes. It is about the ratings."

"When do I get to be real again?"

Annie was more confused as ever. "Real?"

"We call this a reality show, but it isn't real."

"It was real. It *is* real. What are you talking about? You said you really tried. Lisa tried. What about it wasn't real? It was honest *and* real."

"How honest was it that I was the replacement bride? We didn't tell Lisa. That's not honest."

Annie was at a total loss. "Nicole, where is this coming from?"

"Life is more important than ratings." Nicole felt like she went from flying high to hitting the ground face first. She thought she was done with all this. She was with Annie now, not Lisa. She didn't want to sit by Lisa, hold her hand and answer more stupid, personal questions. Why didn't Annie, of all people, understand that? Especially after Annie saw how upsetting it was to be followed for miles by those reporters.

"Ratings *are* life," Annie replied.

Oh no she didn't. She can't believe that. "Where does that leave us then?" Nowhere. That's where it left them. If ratings were life, then Annie could have her ratings. But Nicole didn't want any part of it. "What do I even mean to you? Am I more than just bride number two?"

Annie's eyebrows went up and came down almost meeting in the middle. "Of course. I hired you for your computer skills—"

"That's not what I asked. You hired me. I'm your employee. I was a replacement bride. And I want to be done with this."

"Done with what?"

"All of it. The show. Everything."

"Are you quitting?"

"Yes," Nicole said before she had a chance to think. She turned and walked out of Annie's office and kept going until she was out of the building. She burst into tears as she reached her car. What the hell had just happened? Annie cared more about the ratings than she cared about her? She never saw this coming. *She* mattered more than this damn show. If Annie couldn't see that, then the hell with her. The hell with this job. How could everything go so wrong in an instant? Damn it.

She started her car and drove without caring what direction she was going in. She just needed to drive. To think. To not think. Because, right now, thinking hurt. She found herself in front of Marley's work. She called her from the car. "Umm. Marley. Hey there. What time are you taking lunch?"

"Nicole? Are you okay? Are you sick or have you been crying?"

Having a best friend who knew you so well could be both a blessing and a curse. "I'm not sick."

"Why are you crying? What's going on?"

"What time is your lunch break?" Nicole repeated.

"Where are you?"

"In your parking lot."

"What? I'll be right down." The line went dead.

"No. Marley?" Nicole put her phone on the dashboard. "I didn't mean to interrupt your work," she said to no one.

Nicole jumped when Marley knocked on the passenger window. She wiped the tears from her cheeks. "I didn't mean for you—"

"Just unlock the door." Marley pointed downward.

Nicole did as she asked, and Marley slid onto the seat. "Oh, honey, what's happened?"

"It's Annie."

"I thought things were going good." Marley wiped a fresh tear from Nicole's cheek.

"I thought so too. But apparently her precious show is more important than me."

"Did she say that?"

"She wants me to do more interviews." Nicole shook her head and rubbed her temples. A headache was creeping in. Fast. Why didn't Annie understand that Nicole had done her part? She didn't want to do it anymore.

"And...?"

"And nothing. Marley, reporters are always after me. People stop me on the street. I can't go to a restaurant. And God forbid I go out in public with Annie. This isn't what I signed up for. This isn't the life I want."

"Do you love her?"

Nicole clenched her jaw. "What does that have to do with anything?"

Marley reached over and tucked a stray piece of hair behind Nicole's ear. "Just answer the question."

"It doesn't matter how I feel, because Annie obviously means more to me than I do to her."

"Just because she wants you to do interviews?"

"It's more than that. She puts the show ahead of my feelings. Hell, she puts the show ahead of everything. Everything."

"Didn't you do the same thing?"

Nicole started to object, but Marley held up a hand, stopping her. "Just hear me out. Your job was so important to you that you agreed to marry a total stranger to make sure you didn't lose it."

Nicole thought about it for several long seconds. It wasn't just her job she was afraid of losing. It was Annie too. What a way to try to hang on to someone—by marrying someone else. She laughed out loud at the thought of how ridiculous it all was.

Marley tilted her head and squinted her eyes. "You're laughing now. I'm all kinds of confused here."

"Me too. I have all these..." She waved her hands around. "Feelings. I thought Annie did too. I feel like she used me to make sure her show succeeded."

"I don't think that's true. Isn't the show doing good?"

Nicole nodded.

"And Annie was still into you. Doesn't that prove your theory wrong?"

"I thought so, but today..." Nicole shook her head. "Today, Marley, she was different. I don't know. It hurt. It's over. I quit my job."

"What? Why? It got that bad?"

"I don't know. It seemed that bad in the moment. She basically said the ratings were more important than me." A fresh round of tears cascaded down Nicole's cheeks. She swiped them away. "She said ratings are life."

"What does that mean?" Marley asked.

"It means the *ratings* are her life. I don't fit into that scenario. She can take the ratings and shove them up her ass."

"Nicole, this isn't like you."

And Marley was right. It wasn't. But she was hurt, damn it. Annie meant the world to her. To find out it was all one-sided tore her heart out. "Life is more important than a damn reality show. *I'm* more important. Reality, my ass."

"Tell me how you really feel. Don't hold back now," Marley said.

Nicole laughed, despite her heartache. "Thank you."

"For what?"

"For being you. For leaving work to take care of me."

"Being me is the easy part. I look in the mirror every morning and there I am. Leaving work is a different story. Actually, my boss is out of town this week, so we are kind of running wild in there." She took Nicole's hand. "What are you going to do now?"

"Damned if I know."

❖

Annie's head was reeling. What the hell had just happened? She plopped down in her chair and spun it around to face the window.

Nicole didn't want to do any more interviews. That much was clear. But why had she become so hostile over it? Annie ran the conversation through her head again. Yes, of course ratings were important. But not as important as Nicole had become to her. She failed to make that clear. Not that Nicole had given her much of a chance. Being followed by that reporter a few nights back must have had a profound effect on Nicole. Much more than Annie had realized.

She thought back to that evening. To the intimacy they'd shared. Her body reacted to the memory almost as strongly as it had reacted to Nicole touching her.

"Oh my God." She sat upright in her chair. "I said that ratings are life." That was what sent Nicole over the edge. Of course. Annie hadn't explained. Didn't really get a chance to. She never dreamed it would be taken the way Nicole had obviously taken it. She meant the ratings were the life—the life blood—of the show. They weren't *her* life.

She'd been so thrown by Nicole's response to doing more interviews that she'd messed things up. Why didn't she just accept Nicole's reluctance and drop it? The ratings were good enough without the interviews. The next season's contract was signed with the network. Annie had blown it. She needed a way to explain—to make up for her inconsideration. To get Nicole back. But how?

They were far enough into the production of the new season that Nicole could afford to miss a few days of work without it slowing things down. But that wasn't what Annie was worried about. She wanted Nicole back in her arms. In her bed. She was too deeply entrenched in Annie's heart to give up without a fight.

She tried calling Nicole, but it went directly to voice mail and the text she sent went unanswered. She'd really done it this time.

It went on like that for two days. Annie was tempted to drive to her apartment but wanted to give Nicole space. She was surprised when Nicole showed up at the office, box in hand.

"I'm just here to get my stuff, then I'll be out of your way," she said, sounding more like a disgruntled employee than someone who had made such wonderful love to Annie just a few days before.

"Nicole, can we talk? Please."

"I think we've done all the talking I can handle."

"Nicole, please." Annie wasn't above begging. This was too important.

Nicole shook her head, went into her own office, and shut the door. Annie leaned her head against the door and closed her eyes. How was she going to get Nicole to listen to her?

"I'm sorry," she said through the closed door. "You misunderstood what I was saying."

The door suddenly swung open, and Annie almost went headfirst into Nicole. She stopped herself just short of ramming into her.

"Excuse me? *I* misunderstood? You made your point perfectly clear. There was nothing to misunderstand."

Annie cleared her throat. "When I said that the ratings were life, I didn't—"

"That's the part that hurt the most. I don't want to hear any lame excuse." Nicole's voice was barely above a whisper, the pain evident.

"I didn't mean it. I said it wrong. Please let me—"

Nicole put up her hand. "Stop. I can't listen to this right now. I have too much…" She paused. "It's all too much." She grabbed a sweater from the back of her office chair and threw it in the box.

"You aren't even going to give me two weeks' notice?" Annie was grasping at straws trying any way she could think of to get Nicole to stay long enough to explain.

"Of course, it all goes back to that. Back to this fucking show. That's what it's all about for you. That's all it's ever been about."

Annie went from desperate—something she had never been in any situation she could recall—to angry. Now *that* emotion she was familiar with. "That is so not true. If you would just sit your stubborn ass down and let me explain." Her words were harsh even to her own ears. This was the wrong approach and Annie knew it. She just couldn't seem to help it. Why couldn't Nicole see how much she cared for her? It was more than just this damn job and this damn show. Yes, it had started out that way. The show was everything to her. But not anymore. She would give it all up if it meant keeping Nicole.

"I don't need to stand here and listen to this." Nicole took her box and shoved past Annie.

She was shaking by the time she reached her car. The box was tossed haphazardly into the back seat. She wasn't even sure she'd gotten everything, and at this point she didn't care. How could she have been so wrong about Annie? They wanted such different things.

Nicole hadn't gone looking for love, but things had changed when she started working for Annie. The more she got to know her, the more she wanted to know. But she had been right in the first place. Love wasn't for her. It had never worked out in the past and this just proved that it wasn't meant for her in the future.

She was determined to pour herself into her work. Which meant she had to find another job. She would put Annie and *I Do, I Don't* firmly in her past and she wouldn't look back. The season would be over soon. The world would see that she and Lisa weren't meant to be together, and they would be on to the next thing, the next season. That time couldn't come soon enough for Nicole. And as for any reporters asking her questions, she could say without hesitation that there was nothing between her and Annie. Nothing.

The only thing she needed to do now was figure out how to let the feelings for Annie go. Easier said than done. But lesson learned. Don't give your heart to anyone. It never works out the way you want it to.

Once home, she pulled out her laptop and began her search for jobs. She applied to three of them, all of them paid far less than what she was making with Annie. Oh well. Sacrifices had to be made. Her phone pinged out a text. If it was from Annie, she intended to ignore it. But it wasn't. It was from Lisa. She hadn't heard from her since they had done their last interview together. She wondered if Annie had called her pleading her case. If so, Lisa could just go stick it.

Hey there. I miss you. Lunch on Saturday?

Nicole hesitated before answering. She still had no idea if Lisa was working on Annie's behalf. The timing seemed suspicious. *Miss you too. Heard from Annie lately?* She didn't think Lisa would lie to her.

Not for about a week. Why? What's going on?

I'll fill you in on Saturday. What time and where? Nicole answered. They worked out the details, Nicole satisfied that Annie hadn't called her.

Marley called her to see how picking up her stuff from the office went. Nicole gave her the Reader's Digest version.

"Man, I'm so sorry. She doesn't make it easy, does she?"

"Not at all. I don't know what she wants from me." She paused. "I guess I do. She doesn't want to lose the best computer programmer that she's ever had."

"Aren't you the only computer programmer she's ever had?"

Nicole laughed. She could always count on Marley for that. "Oh sure," she responded. "Throw that up in my face."

"But seriously, do you think that's all it is?" Marley asked.

"What else would it be?"

"I think she may really care about you, but her career got in the way."

"I'm not taking a back seat to anyone's career or anything else. I deserve better than that." She *was* better than that. If it meant she spent the rest of her life alone, then so be it. She was fine with that.

"I'm not suggesting you do that. But I'm wondering if maybe you should sit down with her and hear her out."

Nicole shook her head even though Marley couldn't see her. "What good would that do? She is who she is. She's not about to change for me."

"Even if it is only for closure, I think you should hear her out."

Nicole was dead set against the idea. She had closure enough when she shut Annie down today. It was all she needed. Maybe not *all* she needed. But it was all she wanted. Maybe it was all she thought she could have. Worse yet, maybe that's all she thought she deserved.

"I know what you're thinking, and you need to cut it out."

Nicole didn't have to ask her for clarification. She knew Marley had the ability to just about read her mind. And she was right. That kind of thinking got her nowhere. This was Annie's problem not hers. She was the one married to her career and Nicole wasn't about to be her mistress.

"I applied for a few new jobs," Nicole said.

"Way to change the subject."

"Message received and understood. You're right. I'll stop. I'll be the best damn computer programmer for some other company."

"They'll be lucky to have you."

"Damn right they will be."

"As would any woman."

"You can stop that right now. Because I am done with that. All of it." And she meant it. She knew she'd said it before—before Annie—but now she was done for real.

"Okay. Whatever you say. You know I'm here for you."

"I know. And I appreciate it more than you'll ever know. You're the best."

"Don't expect an argument from me on that one," Marley said. "What are you going to do now?"

"Now? Now I think I'm going to take a nap. After that, I don't know. But I'll figure it out."

Chapter Sixteen

Nicole felt funny knocking on Lisa's door after living there for four months. Lisa opened it with a big smile on her face. "Come on in. It's good to see you."

Nicole followed her into the kitchen. "You seem happy. You cut your hair." It was at least four inches shorter. "It looks good on you."

Lisa ran a hand through her dark locks. "Thanks. I am happy. I met someone. I wanted to tell you in person."

Nicole hugged her. "I'm so glad. Tell me all about her. Where did you meet her? When?"

"Sit."

Nicole sat at the table that had become so familiar to her. She felt a gentle nudge on her thigh and looked down as Bruce stopped by to say hello. "Hey, big fella. How have you been? I've missed you."

"I'll bet," Lisa said. "You are probably sleeping much better without eighty pounds of dog lying on your legs."

"I can't say I miss that part. But I do miss him. And you. But I'm so glad you're doing well."

Lisa set about putting food on the table. Sandwich makings, chips, and Lisa's potato salad, always a favorite of Nicole's. It wasn't steak and lobster but—*no, don't go there. Don't think about the dinner at Annie's that she had to heat up after an evening of—no—no—no. Don't go there.* "Everything looks so good." Nicole said. "Now tell me about your woman."

Lisa sat and put a couple of slices of bread on her plate. She slathered them with mustard and added ham and cheese. "She moved in next door a few weeks ago." She laughed. "Imagine that. I go through all the trouble of getting married trying to find Ms. Right and she goes and moves in right next door. Her name is Chloe and Bruce adores her."

"Well, if Bruce says she's okay then she's good in my book, too." It was good to see Lisa so happy. Nicole still felt bad for—well, for everything.

Lisa proceeded to tell Nicole all about her as she poured them each a glass of Sprite. She did sound like a wonderful person. "Tell me what's going on with you. How are things with Annie? The show? I hear the ratings are good."

"Yes. I heard that about the ratings too. I'm not happy about being stopped on the street or all the personal questions people feel like they have a right to ask. Of course, there are the nice people too. The ones that tell you they are rooting for us." She laughed. "If they only knew. Huh?" Nicole helped herself to the bread and fixed herself a sandwich, complete with slices of dill pickles. She knew Lisa got them out just for her. Lisa hated the taste of dill. A large dollop of potato salad on her plate and Nicole's lunch was complete.

"I totally get it. Chloe and I have got to keep everything hush-hush until the show ends, as I'm sure you and Annie do too. I haven't even told my family about her yet. Not until the last show airs. Not crazy about that part. She seems to understand, so that's good. It helps that she's my neighbor. No strange car in my driveway till all hours of the night or into the morning." A bright red blush filled Lisa's cheeks.

"I'm glad you're getting some," Nicole said with a wink. "Lisa, you deserve the best. I mean that."

"You do too. I hope Annie is treating you right."

Annie. Nicole was torn on whether to tell Lisa what happened or not. She didn't want to bring the mood in the room down. She nodded.

"What aren't you telling me?" Lisa asked.

"What?"

"I was married to you for four months—still am legally. I can tell when something is bothering you. You don't have to tell me if you don't want to. It's probably none of my business. But I have two great ears for listening and a shoulder or two if you need it."

"It's just that—" She stopped. "No. Let's not spoil your good news."

"It's not going to spoil anything. I want you to know I'm here for you," Lisa said.

Nicole took a bite of potato salad and chewed slowly contemplating how much to say. She swallowed and looked at Lisa.

Lisa raised her eyebrows. Waiting.

"Annie seems to care more about the show than me. We broke up." There it was. Plain and simple. Only it wasn't. It was anything but simple. So many feelings had been wrapped up in her and the job that Nicole was still trying to untangle them.

"Oh, Nicole. I'm so sorry. Is it hard to still work for her and see her every day?"

Nicole scrunched her face. "Guess I left out the part about quitting too. Huh?"

"Umm. Yeah, you did. Sounds like your whole life got upended. What can I do to help?"

"Just knowing you care helps." And it did. Knowing she had the support of Marley and Lisa did make her feel better. Less alone. She hadn't told anyone else but figured that Marley had more than likely told Ted.

"Annie is the loser in this situation. She not only lost the best girlfriend she could have had—and this is coming from your wife—she also lost a great programmer."

Nicole laughed. It felt good. "How do you know that I'm a great programmer?" She took a bite of her sandwich, letting the juice from the pickle envelop her mouth and taste buds.

"I know you. I doubt you do anything halfway."

Nicole couldn't argue. She did her job so completely that she ended up with a wife. She was so glad she could now count that wife as a friend. "I doubt Annie will miss me. She has her show to keep her warm at night."

"Do I sense a little bitterness there?"

"Maybe a lot of bitterness." She had a lot to be bitter for. She wasn't going to apologize for it.

"You know what they say. You can either be bitter or be better."

"I don't know who *they* are, but I'm going to be bitter for a while, then I'll be better." Probably a long while.

"They, I believe, are the people who have never been wronged. So, their opinion doesn't count anyway. You be however you need to be for as long as you need."

"You know if you weren't so enthralled with your new neighbor, I might ask you to marry me. You are the perfect woman." Nicole batted her eyes playfully.

"Hey. You had your chance. You blew it, baby."

"I did. Didn't I?"

"We weren't meant to be anything other than friends. We both know that."

Nicole nodded. "I do."

"Last time you said that to me we were standing at the altar. Let's not do that again. At least with each other."

"I don't plan on doing it again with anyone."

"Oh, come on now. It wasn't that bad," Lisa said with a smirk.

"Being married to you was the highlight of my life. Being hurt by Annie hasn't been too much fun. I don't ever want a repeat performance."

"That's understandable. But one relationship gone bad doesn't mean you're doomed for life." Lisa took the last bite of her sandwich and washed it down with soda.

"None of my relationships have worked out."

"That just means you haven't met the right woman yet."

Nicole shook her head. "I really thought Annie was the right one." And she was wrong. Again. Why bother looking if it always ends the same way? With your heart in pieces. "Did Annie call you about doing interviews?"

"No. Did she ask you?"

"Yeah. That's what set this whole thing off. I said no and she didn't like it. I told her it wasn't fair to either of us. She wanted us to do it together. I hope you don't mind that I wouldn't do it."

"I know they aren't your thing. They don't bother me. But if she asks me to do it alone would that be okay with you?"

"Whatever works for you. I don't know if she would want you to do it alone. I mean, not that you're not totally capable, but I think the point is to show a united front. Let the viewers think that everything is hunky-dory between us?"

"Hunky dory?" Lisa laughed. "What?"

Nicole joined in. "Sorry. It's something my mom always says. It means—"

"I got the gist of it."

Nicole scooped more potato salad onto her plate. She really did miss Lisa's cooking. She rarely cooked anything decent just for herself. Her meals usually consisted of fast food or cheese and crackers. It wasn't like she had steak and lobster by herself. No, that privilege was saved for dinners with—stop. Why did her brain keep going back to her perfect evening with Annie? As much as she missed Lisa and her cooking, she missed Annie more.

❖

Annie was at a total loss. She knew if she could just get Nicole to listen to her, to allow her to explain, she could get her back. The void she left at work hurt far less than the void she'd left in Annie's heart.

She'd hardly slept and barely eaten since the misunderstanding. And that's exactly what it was. She failed to express her true feelings about Nicole accurately. Why couldn't she have just said she loved Nicole and that she was more important than any show?

She sat at her desk on a Sunday morning, trying to catch up on the work she'd neglected the last few days. It wasn't that she hadn't tried, but she found herself staring at her computer, her thoughts going again and again to Nicole.

She was going to need help figuring this one out. It was something she'd never asked for before. Ms. Independent needed her sister's help, just like she did when they were kids. She sent her a text. *I could use some advice. Got any free time today to get together?*

She didn't have to wait long for a response. *Great timing. Dean is playing golf today. Want to come over?*

On my way. Annie shut her computer down, grabbed her keys, and headed down to her car. She was sitting in her sister's kitchen within twenty minutes, a glass of ice water sitting in front of her on the table. The plate of cheese and crackers her sister set out sat untouched.

"What are you going to do?" Terry asked after Annie explained what had transpired.

"I don't know. That's why I'm here. I thought maybe you would have some advice. I know you and Dean have had your ups and downs. How do you get through it?" Annie ran a hand through her hair.

"When we fight, it's usually Dean's fault. So, I just give him the silent treatment until he sees the error of his ways and apologizes."

"I guess in this scenario I'm Dean. I've tried to apologize and explain. She won't listen to me. How do I get her to listen?"

"That's a tough one. You may need to trick her to get her in the same space. Dean and I live in the same house so it's impossible not to be in the same space."

Annie shook her head. "I'm not going to trick her. I need to be upfront. Transparent. She means so much to me. I need her to hear that. To absorb it. To believe it."

"What if you went to her house and asked her to hear you out? I mean, she was upset when it happened and upset when she cleaned out her office. Give her a few more days to settle down and then go see her."

"You think *time* is the key?"

"I know I need time when I'm angry."

"How much time?"

"I don't think there is a magic number. Have you ever seen her this upset before?"

Annie thought about it. "No. Not angry. She was upset when she was followed by reporters."

"And you asked her to do more interviews after she already felt violated. Can you see how that would be a problem for her?"

Annie saw that now. She didn't realize it at the time. "Yes." She would have never set up more interviews if she'd known. She had been clueless and that might be unforgivable.

"Do you think it would help if you talked to someone who is close to Nicole? Are she and Lisa still close? Or does she have siblings?"

Annie thought about if for several long moments. Would it make it better or worse if she talked to Marley? Would Marley even talk to her? Annie was sure that Nicole had already told her

her side of the story. Marley probably already thought Annie was an ass. But maybe it was worth a try. She had to do something to get Nicole to listen to her. "She has a sister-in-law she's close to." She paused. "What if it backfires and Nicole hates me even more?"

"I don't think she hates you. She's hurt. She thinks she doesn't matter to you as much as you matter to her. If she didn't have strong feelings for you, she wouldn't have taken this so hard."

Annie hadn't thought of it in those terms before. This whole thing had her brain in a jumble. It was so unlike her to let a problem become so all consuming. But this wasn't just any problem. It was one that could affect the rest of her life. She'd never wanted anyone to be her forever as much as she wanted Nicole.

"I think you should talk to her sister-in-law. It may be the only way."

"I hope you're right." Annie stood.

"Where are you going?" Terry asked.

"Back to the office."

"Annie, more work—"

Annie held up her hand. "Not more work. I'm done throwing myself into my work to avoid having a real life. Marley, Nicole's sister-in-law's number is at the office. Luckily, she was her maid of honor."

Terry rose and gave Annie a hug. "Good luck. Let me know how it goes."

"I will." *Please, dear God, let this work.* She didn't know what else to do if it didn't.

❖

Annie ran her hand through her hair. Her stomach was in knots, and she couldn't remember the last time she'd been this nervous. She typed Marley's number into her phone, praying she would answer. She did.

"Marley? Hi. It's Annie, from—"

"I know who you are," Marley said. Annie couldn't quite read her tone of voice.

"I'm sure you know what happened between Nicole and myself."

"I do." Annie could hear her guard go up, even over the phone.

"I messed up." No sense beating around the bush. Time to lay it all out on the table. "Marley, I love her. I said some things that Nicole took wrong. I should have explained things better."

Silence.

"She won't talk to me. I need to tell her how I feel. She is more important to me than anything else in this world." Annie let out a deep breath.

"Even your precious show?" Marley asked.

"That's a fair question and the answer is yes. I love her more than this show. More than anything else. I would give up this production company if it meant getting Nicole back." And she would. She didn't think it would come to that, but if it did, she would choose Nicole over anything else.

"How am I supposed to believe you? Nicole has been a mess over this."

"All I can give you is my word. Nicole means the world to me." Annie paced back and forth across the carpet.

"What do you want from me?" Marley's voice softened.

"Can you help me talk to her? Maybe get us in the same place or talk to her for me? I don't know. I need her to know how I feel. If she rejects me after that, then I'll let her go. But, Marley, I'll never be able to live with myself knowing how much I hurt her and her not knowing the truth."

"Give me some time to think about it. If I do it, I'm doing it for Nicole. Not for you."

"Understood. I only want the best for her, too."

It was two days before she heard back from Marley. "Can you come to my house today at two? I mean I know that's in the middle of your workday, but that's when Nicole will be here."

Annie's heart pounded so hard in her chest that she was sure Marley would be able to hear it through the phone. "Of course."

Marley gave her the address and Annie typed it into the GPS app on her phone. "I'll be there. Thank you, Marley."

"Just don't hurt her," Marley responded. "Or I'm going to have to break both your legs."

"I won't. I promise." Annie suddenly felt like she was going to throw up.

She was given a chance to make things right. She was grateful and scared. She could only pray that Nicole would listen and believe her. She shut down her computer. There was no way she could concentrate on work. She had almost three hours to go before she needed to head to Marley's.

She called Terry, knowing that she might not be able to answer her phone at work. To her surprise, she did answer. "You've got this," Terry said after Annie explained what had transpired. "Be calm, state your case, and give her time to absorb it."

Annie had never felt so helpless. The fate of her future rested in Nicole's hands. The hands that had caressed her body so lovingly, so recently that Annie could still feel them.

"Listen, I need to get back to work. Call me tonight and let me know how it went."

Annie agreed and hung up. She headed out, stopping at Lace's office. "I'm leaving," she told her.

"For the day?"

"Probably. You can leave anytime you want. You'll still get paid for a full day."

Lace obviously knew that Nicole had quit, there was no hiding the fact that she no longer came in to work, but Annie hadn't shared the details of their breakup and mercifully, Lace hadn't asked.

"You okay, boss?"

"Hopefully, I will be soon." She didn't offer an explanation. She drove around aimlessly until it was time to head to Marley's. She didn't know what else to do with herself. Thoughts about what she wanted to say and how she wanted to say it swirled endlessly through her head. She couldn't make it stop.

She wanted to start by saying how much she loved Nicole but knew that wasn't a good idea. She'd done enough research for the show to know that if the other person didn't return those feelings, it could make them run. Hell, she'd experienced it in her own life, when someone said it too soon.

Nicole's car was in Marley's driveway when Annie arrived. She took three deep breaths, exited her car, and forced herself to walk to the door and ring the bell.

Nicole had been surprised when Marley called, inviting her to a late lunch, especially on a day that Marley would usually be working. She'd just finished her pizza when the doorbell rang. Marley rushed to answer it.

Nicole was both shocked and a little pissed when she saw Annie walk into the kitchen. If she was being honest with herself, she was also happy to see her. She knew she missed her but didn't realize how much until that moment. She pushed down the desire to hug her. To feel Annie's arms around her in return. She was on her feet, eyes locked on Marley. "What's going on?"

Marley put up her hands. "Before you get mad at me, just hear what Annie has to say."

"You helped her plan this?" Nicole didn't know if she should be madder at Annie or at Marley. "This is an ambush."

"No, it's not," Marley assured her. "You two need to talk. For both your sakes." She looked from one to the other. "I've got to go back to work. Nicole, please lock up when you leave. And

I trust the two of you will play nice and I won't come home to a busted window or shattered TV." She grabbed a bottle of Pepsi from the fridge and headed out the door, leaving Nicole alone with Annie.

"I don't appreciate you using my friends to get to me," Nicole said.

"It was the only way I could think of to get you to talk to me. I'm sorry."

"And what exactly are you sorry for?" Nicole didn't try to hide the anger—or was it hurt—in her voice.

"Everything. Can we sit down, so I can explain?"

Nicole figured the sooner she heard Annie out the sooner this would be over. She led the way to the living room and sat in the rocker, forcing Annie to sit on the couch by herself. It wouldn't be safe to be too close to her. Too many feelings still existed in Nicole's heart for that.

"You, Nicole Hart, are more important to me than the show. Than anything. Than my career. If you asked me to give it all up, I would. For you. I would deal with the fallout, the lawsuit from the network, whatever. For you."

Her words sounded good, but it was the other words she had said that broke her heart that mattered. "You said the ratings were your life."

Annie shook her head. "No. I said the ratings *were* life."

Semantics. It all meant the same thing. "There's no difference."

"There is a huge difference." Annie's voice was calm. Soothing. "I meant the ratings were life to the show. Not to me." She paused and seemed to be gathering her thoughts. "Yes. The show—my career, used to be everything to me. It was my whole life. I didn't leave room for anything or anyone else. But that changed. That changed, Nicole, when I realized I had feelings for you." She got up, crossed the small distance between them, and knelt in front of Nicole, looking up at her. "You changed me. Made me want more for myself than work. Made me want you."

Nicole didn't know what to think. Was it possible she had misinterpreted Annie's words that day at the office? "What about the interviews? You knew what that would do to me. You knew."

"I didn't. And that's on me. I knew how upset you were when that reporter followed you. I thought in a controlled environment you would be okay. That I would make sure you were okay. In that moment, yes, I was thinking about the success of the show. But I never would have pushed you, and I never called Lisa to do the interviews after what you said. You showed me what matters most."

"And what is that?" Nicole's heart was starting to soften despite her attempts to keep a wall around it.

"You. You are what matters most. And Lisa too. Without realizing it I was using the two of you like pawns for the success of the show. I won't make that mistake again. With you, with Lisa, or with anyone else who chooses to be on future shows."

"How do I know that what you're telling me is true?" Nicole wasn't willing to give in without being sure. As much as she wanted Annie—and that was one hell of a lot—she couldn't risk being hurt again.

Annie took her hand. She was trembling. Nervous. Nicole had never seen her like this before. It knocked down any of the remaining bricks surrounding her heart. "Look into my eyes and you'll know the truth." Annie's eyes were filled with tears, tears that cascaded down her cheeks with a simple blink. There was also truth there. And something else. The way Annie looked at her, there was no mistaking the feeling behind it. "I will do whatever it takes to make this up to you. If you want to come back to work, I'll make you an executive producer with the power to override me if you think I'm being unethical. I want you back, Nicole. Back in my life. Back in my arms. Please."

Nicole's heart melted with those last words. But it was all too much to take in at once. She needed time. Needed to sort through her own feelings. She believed what Annie was telling her, but she needed more. She just wasn't sure what that *more* was at the moment.

"Say something. Please. If you want me to go to hell I will. But to be honest, that's where I've been since my words sent you running."

"I don't want you to go to hell. I want you to go home or back to work or wherever right now. I need time. I need space." *I need to be away from you before I start kissing you.* Jumping back in with both feet wasn't a good idea. And if she dipped in a toe—well, that would just lead to the jumping.

"Okay," Annie said. The edge of sadness in her voice made Nicole want to wrap her in her arms and never let her go.

No. Let her go. Take time to think. To be sure.

Annie got up and walked to the door. She turned back to Nicole, hand on the doorknob. "Everything I said here is true. You mean the world to me, Nicole. I'm willing to shout it out to the world. No more hiding. Even if it means the end of the show. And even if you never forgive me, I want you to know that." She turned and left, leaving a void in the space she'd just occupied.

The void felt like it could swallow Nicole whole. Yes, she believed Annie. Yes, she wanted her back. Was it that simple? Could she possibly have what she didn't think she could have? Love.

She sat there for a long time contemplating her choices. She could *lose* it all, her job, her chances with Annie, or she could *have* it all. It was an easy decision to make.

Chapter Seventeen

A nnie was shocked to see Nicole in her office when she got there Monday morning. She wasn't sure if she was there because she came back to work or because she was just collecting whatever else she may have left there. She was afraid to find out and wasn't sure how to ask or even if she should.

Nicole looked up and caught her eye. "Oh, hi. Thought I would get a jump-start on the day and catch up on the work I missed last week."

What the hell? She was back. Annie couldn't help but smile. She didn't know what it meant for the two of them, but it was a good start. A great start.

"It's wonderful to see you," Annie said.

Nicole returned her smile. "Good to be back. I thought maybe we could have a little meeting in your office later."

Annie assumed she wanted to talk about her offer to make Nicole a producer. If that's what she wanted, Annie would be happy to do that. "Sure thing. Just let me know whenever you're ready."

Nicole nodded and placed her attention back on her computer.

Annie felt like she floated back to her own office. She had no idea if Nicole was willing to give them another chance, but they could take their time to work toward that as long as she was willing.

She had just started going through her notes for the day when there was a knock on her door. She looked up, expecting it to be Lace. "Come on in."

Nicole sauntered in, closed the door behind her, and leaned against it. "Okay if we have that meeting now?"

Annie leaned back in her chair. "Of course." She was prepared to give Nicole anything she asked for. The producer title. A raise. Her left kidney.

She was surprised when Nicole locked the door, came toward her, and perched on the edge of her desk, facing her. Several long moments of silence passed between them.

"I'm just wondering if you're ever going to kiss me again," Nicole said at last.

"What?" Annie didn't know what else to say.

"I'm just wondering—"

Annie was on her feet in a split second. "I heard you," she said before crashing her mouth into Nicole's. She wrapped her arms around Nicole and let the euphoria of being this close to her again surround her. She was breathless by the time she came up for air. "Does this mean you forgive me?"

"I'm working on it."

"What else do I need to do?"

Nicole spun them around, so Annie was leaning against the desk. "Take off your pants."

"What?"

"Let me spell it out. Take off your pants. Sit on the desk and spread your legs."

Annie's body reacted to Nicole's words, and she felt her underwear soaked with her desire.

"If you want to," Nicole added. "It's all about consent. I don't want you to feel pressured."

"The pressure's building all right, but you have my full consent."

Nicole unzipped her pants before Annie had a chance to. She squatted and pulled them down to Annie's ankles, followed by her underwear. She buried her face in Annie's center.

"Wait," Annie managed to squeak out. She wasn't sure her legs would hold her up, they were trembling uncontrollably.

Nicole stood, grabbed Annie by the waist, and lifted her to the desk. "Okay?"

Annie nodded, sure that if she attempted to speak no words would come out.

Nicole ran a single finger through Annie's folds. "Mmm. I've missed you," she whispered.

Annie let out a groan and gripped Nicole's shoulders, afraid she might float right off the desk.

Nicole captured her lips once again, slipping two very skilled fingers inside her. Annie rocked against her as much as her limited position would allow. But Nicole was doing enough moving for both of them, as her fingers slipped in and out of Annie, bringing her to the edge of an orgasm and then backing off just enough to let the tension ease.

Annie had never begged for release in her life, but she was about to now. She wrenched their mouths apart. "Please," she said.

Nicole slipped a third finger in and increased the speed and pressure. "How's this?" she asked.

Annie closed her eyes and threw her head back in response. She was so close. Without warning, Nicole dropped to her knees and ran her tongue between Annie's wet folds. Annie's orgasm burst from her center, through her chest and out her head. She felt like every part of her was involved in the explosion. The pressure from Nicole's fingers between her legs stayed constant until she came down from the cloud she had landed on.

She sucked in a breath as Nicole eased her fingers out and stood. "I'm baaack," Nicole said in a singsong voice.

Annie opened her eyes and blinked against the tears that had built up in them. She wasn't even close to being able to respond. Her breath came in ragged bursts. She could only nod.

"I thought you would be happy to see me." She faked a frown. "And now you won't even talk to me? I guess I deserve that. There was a while there when I wouldn't talk to you. But I'm so glad I eventually did. Because…" She hesitated. "Because," she continued. "I'm in love with you, Annie Jackson. And just for the record, I never thought I would ever say those words to anyone. Ever. But I do, Annie. I love you. Even changed your ringtone to 'Love of My Life.'"

"By Queen?" Annie asked.

"Jim Brickman."

"Much better." Annie smiled. "Me too. I love you too."

"Isn't this romantic?" Nicole said through a wide smile. "Doing it on your desk? Makeup sex is the best. Isn't it?"

"You're the best." The throbbing between Annie's legs was just starting to subside.

"Are you sure you aren't just riding the high of an orgasm?" Nicole teased her.

"I was in love with you before that incredible orgasm," Annie responded. "Did I mention it was incredible?"

Nicole kissed her nose. "I believe you did. Yes."

"Does this mean you'll be my girlfriend?"

"Well…" Nicole tapped her chin. "I don't make a habit of doing this kind of thing with strangers. So, I think it does."

"I'm so glad. I missed you so much."

"I'm sorry," Nicole said.

"What are you apologizing for? I'm the one who messed everything up."

"But we could have been doing this sooner if I had been willing to listen to you."

"You're right. It was all your fault. I accept your apology and I am grateful for the way you decided to make it up to me," Annie responded.

"Good. Now where do we go from here?"

"Too soon to ask you to marry me?" Annie said, only half kidding.

"Yes. I jumped into marriage way too soon last time. I'd like to take it a little slower this time around. But keep that question in your back pocket for the future. Because you never know."

"Oh, I know," Annie said. "With you. I know."

About the Author

Creativity for Joy Argento started young. She was only five, growing up in Syracuse, New York, when she picked up a pencil and began drawing animals. These days she calls Rochester home, and oil paints are her medium of choice. Her award-winning art has found its way into homes around the globe.

Writing came later in life for Joy. Her love of lesbian romance inspired her to try her hand at writing, and she found her first self-published novels well received. She is thrilled to be a part of the Bold Strokes family and has enjoyed their books for years.

Joy has three grown children who are making their own way in the world and six grandsons who are the light of her life.

Books Available from Bold Strokes Books

A Second Chance at Life by Genevieve McCluer. Vampires Dinah and Rachel reconnect, but a string of vampire killings begin and evidence seems to be pointing at Dinah. They must prove her innocence while finding out if the two of them are still compatible after all these years. (978-1-63679-459-4)

Digging for Heaven by Jenna Jarvis. Litz lives for dragons. Kella lives to kill them. The last thing they expect is to find each other attractive. (978-1-63679-453-2)

Forever's Promise by Missouri Vaun. Wesley Holden migrated west disguised as a man for the hope of a better life and with no designs to take a wife, but Charlotte Rose has other ideas. (978-1-63679-221-7)

Here For You by D. Jackson Leigh. A horse trainer must make a difficult business decision that could save her father's ranch from foreclosure but destroy her chance to win the heart of a feisty barrel racer vying for a spot in the National Rodeo Finals. (978-1-63679-299-6)

I Do, I Don't by Joy Argento. Creator of the romance algorithm, Nicole Hart doesn't expect to be starring in her own reality TV dating show, and falling for the show's executive producer Annie Jackson could ruin everything. (978-1-63679-420-4)

It's All in the Details by Dena Blake. Makeup artist Lane Donnelly and wedding planner Helen Trent can't stand each other, but they must set aside their differences to ensure Darcy gets the wedding of her dreams, and make a few of their own dreams come true. (978-1-63679-430-3)

Marigold by Melissa Brayden. Marigold Lavender vows to take down Alexis Wakefield, the harsh food critic who blasts her younger sister's restaurant. If only she wasn't as sexy as she is mean. (978-1-63679-436-5)

The Town that Built Us by Jesse J. Thoma. When her father dies, Grace Cook returns to her hometown and tries to avoid Bonnie Whitlock, the woman who pulverized her heart, only to discover her father's estate has been left to them jointly. (978-1-63679-439-6)

A Degree to Die For by Karis Walsh. A murder at the University of Washington's Classics Department brings Professor Antigone Weston and Sergeant Adriana Kent together—first as opposing forces, and then allies as they fight together to protect their campus from a killer. (978-1-63679-365-8)

A Talent Within by Suzanne Lenoir. Evelyne, born into nobility, and Annika, a peasant girl with a deadly secret, struggle to change their destinies in Valmora, a medieval world controlled by religion, magic, and men. (978-1-63679-423-5)

Finders Keepers by Radclyffe. Roman Ashcroft's past, it seems, is not so easily forgotten when fate brings her and Tally Dewilde together—along with an attraction neither welcomes. (978-1-63679-428-0)

Homeland by Kristin Keppler and Allisa Bahney. Dani and Kate have finally found themselves on the same side of the war, but a new threat from the inside jeopardizes the future of the wasteland. (978-1-63679-405-1)

Just One Dance by Jenny Frame. Will Taylor Spark and her new business to make dating special—the Regency Romance Club—bring sparkle back to Jaq Bailey's lonely world? (978-1-63679-457-0)

On My Way There by Jaycie Morrison. As Max traverses the open road, her journey of impossible love, loss, and courage mirrors her voyage of self-discovery leading to the ultimate question: If she can't have the woman of her dreams, will the woman of real life be enough? (978-1-63679-392-4)

Transitioning Home by Heather K O'Malley. An injured soldier realizes they need to transition to really heal. (978-1-63679-424-2)

Truly Enough by JJ Hale. Chasing the spark of creativity may ignite a burning romance or send a friendship up in flames. (978-1-63679-442-6)

Vintage and Vogue by Kelly and Tana Fireside. When tech whiz Sena Abrigo marches into small-town Owen Station, she turns librarian Hazel Butler's life upside down in the most wonderful of ways, setting off an explosive series of events, threatening their chance at love...and their very lives. (978-1-63679-448-8)

Broken Fences by Jo Hemmingwood. Former army sergeant Seneca Twist has difficulty adjusting to civilian life until she meets psychologist Robyn Mason and has a place to call home. (978-1-63679-414-3)

Never Kiss a Cowgirl by Ali Vali. Asher Evans dreams of winning the National Finals Rodeo in Vegas, and Reagan Wilson wants no part of something that brings back the memory of what killed her father. (978-1-63679-106-7)

Pantheon Girls by Jean Copeland. Cassie Burke never anticipated the detour life was about to take when a meeting with a prospective client reunites her with a past love and reignites the star-crossed passion they shared twenty years earlier. (978-1-63679-337-5)

Roux for Two by Aurora Rey. For TV chef Chelsea Boudreaux and hometown boy Bryce Cormier, love proves as tricky as making a good pot of gumbo. (978-1-63679-376-4)

Starting Over by Nance Sparks. Jennifer has no idea if she can mend Sam's broken soul after the sudden loss of her wife, but it's never too late for starting over. (978-1-63679-409-9)

The Accidental Bride by Jane Walsh. Spinsters Miss Grace Linfield and Miss Thea Martin travel to Gretna Green to prevent a wedding, only to discover a scandalous passion—for each other. (978-1-63679-345-0)

Three Wishes by Anne Shade. A magic lamp, a beautiful Jinni, and a cursed princess make for one unbelievable story. (978-1-63679-349-8)

Undiscovered Treasures by MJ Williamz. For Cyl and her friends Luna and Martinique, life's best treasures often appear when you're not looking. (978-1-63679-449-5)

Curse of the Gorgon by Tanai Walker. Cass will do anything to ensure Elle's safety, but is she willing to embrace the curse of the Gorgon? (978-1-63679-395-5)

Dance with Me by Georgia Beers. Scottie Templeton mixes it up on and off the dance floor with sexy salsa instructor Marisa Reyes. But can Scottie get past Marisa's connection to her ex? (978-1-63679-359-7)

Gin and Bear It by Joy Argento. Opposites really can attract, and as Kelly and Logan work together to create a loving home for rescue cat Bear, they just might find one for themselves as well. (978-1-63679-351-1)

Harvest Dreams by Jacqueline Fein-Zachary. Planting the vineyard of their dreams, Kate Bauer and Sydney Barrett must resist their attraction while battling nature and their families, who oppose both the venture and their relationship. (978-1-63679-380-1)

The No Kiss Contract by Nan Campbell. Workaholic Davy believes she can get the top spot at her firm if the senior partners think she's settling down and about to start a family, but she needs the delightful yet dubious Anna to help by pretending to be her fiancée. (978-1-63679-372-6)

Outside the Lines by Melissa Sky. If you had the chance to live forever, would you take it? Amara Rodriguez did, and it sets her on a journey to find her missing mother and unravel the mystery of her own heart. (978-1-63679-403-7)

The Value of Sylver and Gold by Michelle Larkin. When word gets out that former Boston homicide detective Reid Sylver can talk to the dead, the FBI solicits her help on a serial murder case, prompting Reid to assemble forces once again with Detective London Gold. (978-1-63679-093-0)

When It Feels Right by Tagan Shepard. Freshly out of the closet Marlene hasn't been lucky in love, but when it comes to her quirky new roommate Abby, everything just feels right. (978-1-63679-367-2)